Henry William Pullen

Tom Pippin's Wedding

A Novel

Henry William Pullen

Tom Pippin's Wedding
A Novel

ISBN/EAN: 9783337031718

Printed in Europe, USA, Canada, Australia, Japan

Cover: Foto ©Andreas Hilbeck / pixelio.de

More available books at **www.hansebooks.com**

TOM PIPPIN'S WEDDING.

A NOVEL.

BY THE AUTHOR OF

"THE FIGHT AT DAME EUROPA'S SCHOOL."

PHILADELPHIA:

J. B. LIPPINCOTT & CO.

1871.

CONTENTS.

(v)

TOM PIPPIN'S WEDDING.

INTRODUCTORY CHAPTER.

A WORD ABOUT BOY-FARMING.

A SENSATION NOVEL. Three murders, two bigamies, a forgery, and a theft. A five days' trial of the
innocent heroine, found guilty at last by twelve pig-
headed jurymen of her country, and sentenced to death,
amid the awful stillness of the Court, by a mean little
judge in spectacles, whose voice falters with suppressed
emotion, and who afterwards gets very properly extinguished by the Home Secretary and the Author for
being such an old idiot as to sum up against the interesting prisoner at the bar.

*   *   *   *   *   *

Two forms emerge at midnight in November from
the dark recesses of a copse, where they had lain concealed for hours, and where any one else but a house-
breaker would, to say the least, have caught a very
severe cold in the head. Creeping stealthily through
the tangled brushwood, lest the numerous passers-by
at that time of night should hear the twigs crackle, and
catch the muffled sound of their footfall upon the autumn
leaves, they gain at length the threshold of some lordly

domain, where their inevitable accomplice, the butler,
faithless to his trust, draws back the well-greased bolt
and lets them in.   But the master of the house, rest-
less with presentiment of some impending doom, and
seeking a volume from the wainscoted library of his
ancestors, to beguile the weary hour, foils the guilty
purpose of the traitor by accosting him at the bottom
of the staircase with a tragical "Ha! what have we
here?"

＊　　＊　　＊　　＊　　＊　　＊

The disinherited maiden, stung to madness with a
sense of her cruel wrongs, kneels beside the death-bed
of her stern papa.   He relents not, but swears a fearful
oath that she shall never possess a penny of his wealth.
She, gazing at him with a peculiar light in her dark
eyes, which he remembers to have noticed once before,
flits ghostlike across the chamber, and feels with her
thumb and forefinger for a spot in the paneling of the
wall.   It yields to her soft pressure, and discloses a
secret drawer, with nothing in it.   "Ha!" faintly
cries the dying man, with something of triumph in his
tone.   "Ha, ha!" responds the maiden, searching him
through and through with her expressive orbs; "ha,
ha! remorseless one! 'tis thus, e'en thus, that I thwart
your base designs!"   In the inmost recesses of the
drawer appears to her practiced eye another spring.
She touches it, and lo! a hidden cavity reveals itself,
from whence with trembling hand she snatches the last
will and testament of her unnatural parent.   Deliberately striking a match, warranted only to ignite upon
the box—for the reader is warned that every apparently
insignificant detail of these little freaks at midnight

has some important bearing on the story—she lights the wax-candles on the dressing-table, spreads the parchment out before her, erases with the finely-tempered blade of a penknife the name of her brutal cousin five times removed, and, taking the precaution —you are particularly requested to observe—to dip her pen in the ink, traces with steady hand her own name, and deposits the document again in the secret drawer. The dying man looks on aghast, powerless to hinder the unholy deed; and, in a paroxysm of rage and horror, breathes his last. At that moment the bedstead is seen to rock and heave; its curtains are swayed to and fro as if by some supernatural agency; and the cowering maiden has scarcely time to shriek, when she stands face to face with the majestic figure of her cousin five times removed.

*　　*　　*　　*　　*　　*

This is the sort of thing that a novel-writer of the present age is expected to produce; and upon my word, indulgent reader, I am not equal to it. I am not, indeed. A quiet murder or two I might manage; but bigamies and forgeries at midnight shock me exceedingly. You will excuse me, I am sure, if I try my hand at something less horrible, but not on that account less true to life. What do you say, now, to a little bit of boy-farming? We have heard a good deal lately about Margaret Waters, and the helpless little victims of her cruelty and lust. Few British fathers, certainly not one single British mother, felt anything like pity for the wretched woman, when the news came down that she had "paid the last penalty of the law." But are you innocent of the fact, O fond mamma, that the dear boy whom you have intrusted to the keeping of the Reverend Mr. Deemon, to be instructed, bedded, and boarded, for thirty, forty, fifty pounds a year, is as literally farmed by his master, and put out to grass by his mistress, as any base-born infant in the sunny pastures of Holloway or the Seven Dials? You don't believe it? Very well. You had better pay a visit to some private academy or grammar-school, and see.

How do you suppose that schoolmasters and school-mistresses make their money and retire? Why, by stale bread that the wretched children cannot chew; and rancid butter, of which a little goes a surprisingly long way; and the nasty parts of the sheep or cow which the butcher can't get any one else to take off his hands; and a draughty school-room without a fire on a damp October night, to save sixpennyworth of coal, and one blanket on the miserable bed, when the poor little boy would have shivered under three.

"Oh, dear, dear, this is very dreadful! Why, you are bringing up Dotheboys Hall over again. I thought Nicholas Nickleby had done away with all that, long ago."

Yes, exactly. Charles Dickens, all honor to him, caricatured the worst type of a Yorkshire school, and public indignation raved and stormed for a month or two, and commissions sat, and justices of the peace talked big, and everybody supposed that we had effected some marvelous reform. It was a genuine English proceeding. A great fuss, a great many letters in the newspapers, a great many meetings, a great step just going to be taken, and then—a great excitement got up about something else.

Trust me, kind father, tender-hearted mother, guardian too upright to do your young charge a wrong; trust me, there is many and many a Dotheboys Hall, where little bodies are starved and shrunk, and little spirits are broken, still. And, so long as you insist upon "doing the thing cheap," so long will such institutions thrive. Schoolmasters and schoolmistresses must live; and, considering their incessant toil and worry, they have need to live well. Let them make their fair profit; and, if a boy cannot be fed for twelve shillings a week, let them ask fifteen. But, in spite of Nicholas Nickleby and its supposed reforms, every schoolmaster who does not love his work devotedly for its own sake, and not for what he can get out of it, is a genuine Wackford Squeers; and every schoolmistress who grinds and screws, and calculates to a fraction how much a head she can save per week by sending out small helpings all round, is as thorough-going a baby-farmer as ever was Mrs. Margaret Waters, and as richly deserves to be—hanged.

Of course there is no palpable cruelty. It would not be tolerated now. We are a great deal too refined. The birch has become a mediæval superstition, and a boy who should be sent home for the holidays with bruises on his back would probably be removed. It is a pity there are no outward and visible signs to be recognized of wounds inflicted elsewhere. It is a pity that there is no tell-tale register of the food, in quality and quantity alike, which the little stomach has taken in, and digests as best it may. It is a pity that there can be no record kept of dirt and damp and neglect; of wet feet, endured night after night, to save servants

the trouble of fetching dry shoes and socks; of head-
aches laughed at, and toothaches misbelieved in, and
coughs and colds left to cure themselves in the rain.
Every now and then the Register does tell its tale,
when some little fellow catches rheumatic fever, and
dies; and then people say that boys will be boys, and
that the urchin deserved a good whipping for lying on
the grass; and the corpse goes home to its mother,
and the young brothers and sisters throw flowers into
the grave; and the Reverend Mr. Deemon preaches a
funeral sermon in the school chapel, and weeps the
tears of a hypocrite over the loss of his boy, and the
tears of a schoolmaster over the loss of his fifty pounds
a year.   There is another Record, too, of all these
things, kept somewhere else, which has yet to be dis-
closed; and, when the accounts of that Book are
balanced, few of us would like to change places with
the Reverend Mr. Deemon.

It is not of the slightest use, O green, very green, papa,
to come and visit your dear boy at school after three
weeks' notice of your arrival.   You may save yourself
the trouble of such an inspection as that, for there will
be nothing to inspect.   Everything will be just as it
should be.   The boys will have a good dinner that
day, and look their happiest as the unwonted dainties
are carried round.   The schoolmaster will have washed
his hands and changed his school-coat; and the schoolmistress will smile with motherly affection, and wear a
nice clean collar.   You will think what a very pre-
possessing couple they are.   But just drop in upon
them some day unawares, and ask for a bit of luncheon
in the dining-hall with the boys.   Oh, no—they could

not think of it. The room has just been painted, and
it smells; or there is something the matter with the
stove. They are quite ashamed to let you see it; but
you shall have a sandwich in the parlor, and join the
boys presently. A very simple-minded gentleman, on
such occasions, is the British father. He believes im-
plicitly any humbug which the schoolmaster pleases to
talk in praise of his establishment; but, if the boy's
account should be somewhat different, the fond parent
becomes suddenly incredulous, and thinks it only
natural that children should abuse their teachers. Why
is it natural? Who made it natural? The fact is, it
is natural for boys to praise those who are kind to
them, and to abuse those who bully them; and much
more natural for the boy to tell the plain truth, and
say whether he is treated well or ill, than for the boy-
farmer to tell the plain truth, when less than half the
truth would empty his school. Natural, indeed! why,
the only opinion about a school worth having is the
opinion of the boys. What do Inspectors know about
it, who come at stated intervals, and find everything
in apple-pie order? What do public Examiners know
about it, for whom each form has been crammed with
half a hundred dates and facts? Examiners, nine-
tenths of whom are so frightfully nervous over their
work that they have scarcely the pluck to put a straight-
forward question before a good big class of boys, much
less to offend the master by making an unfavorable report of his school? "Highly satisfactory, showing a
decided improvement since midsummer." This is the
stereotyped Christmas verdict. Who ever heard of an
Inspector or an Examiner daring to depart from it?

Let these gentlemen look in some day without notice, and watch the master hearing his form. Let them see whether he can make the boys mind him; whether he can keep his temper; whether he knows how to teach; whether he is a judge of character; whether he does his work because he likes it, or because he is paid for it at the rate of so much a head. Let them find out what Mrs. Deemon has got for dinner, for the boys—and for herself. Let them inquire how much of their regulation play-time yonder pale, sickly little fellows spend every day writing impositions, because the master does not know how to make them learn their lessons in school. This is the way to examine and inspect; but, of course, this would not be dignified, this would not be English, this would not be red tape; and, therefore, Examiners shall continue to make their interesting and highly valuable reports, and Inspectors to butter up the schoolmaster.

It will be understood that these observations are directed, not against public schools, for whose system, as in gratitude and duty bound, the author has the highest possible respect; nor against any one school in particular. But they are directed, most emphatically, against all schools, whether private or endowed, wherein the boys are at the mercy of a brute who hates them; who crams them up for examinations to save his own credit, and takes no real trouble to make them learn; who cares nothing for their games or pleasures, and thinks the very sound of their voices in the playground a bore; who drives them like cattle, and knows how to win neither their confidence nor their love; who has undertaken, for filthy lucre's sake, a work which he is

utterly unfit to do; and is responsible to nobody but
his own conscience, which died the melancholy death
of suffocation several years ago. They *are* directed,
these feeble words of mine, against those charming
motherly-looking females, who provide the dear children in the advertisements with the comforts of a
home, and in the dining-hall with fat and gristle and
watery beer; who stroke the little curly head when
mamma comes to see her boy, and pull its hair spite-
fully when she is gone; who have no kindlier remedy
for boyish aches than a powder, and no sympathy for
childish troubles more gracious than a sneer.   There
are hundreds of such men, and thousands of such
women, grinding and squeezing extra fourpences a
week out of hungry little stomachs, as unblushingly as
if Dotheboys Hall had never been painted, and Nicholas Nickleby had not been read by all the world.
Under cover of the admitted fact, that schools are
better managed than they were; that the error of the
present time runs rather in the direction of over-pet-
ting than of ill treatment; and that young people
nowadays have a great deal too much of their own way;
with popular impressions such as these it is uncommonly easy for Mr. and Mrs. Deemon, in their quiet
corner, to administer a wholesome corrective to the
indulgent spirit of the age.   The theory that "boys
are all the better for roughing it," is a highly convenient theory, when you propose to pay for their education the smallest possible amount; and there will
always be plenty of parents to whom it is gratifying to
know that, if their dear child should go every night
empty to bed, he is at any rate in the hands of judi-

cious friends who will never make him sick with excess
of feeding.

Should any schoolmaster do me the honor to read
my little book, I will trust first that what I have said
may clearly not apply to him ;* and secondly, that, if
it does apply to him, he will be more disposed to feed
his boys better, and treat them with greater kindness,
than to abuse my "bad taste," in taking the part of
poor helpless childhood against that innumerable company of bullies, whose profession is boy-farming, and
whose family name is Squeers.

---

* To avoid even the risk of giving personal offense, I think it better
to say positively, what, however, I hope it was unnecessary to say at
all, that I do *not* allude to any educational establishment in or near
Salisbury.

CHAPTER II.

MR. GOGGS DEMONSTRATES HIS LOVE OF BOYS.

THE nursery at Slappingham Vicarage was rather a sight on a Saturday evening. Five little brats, from eight years old and downwards, had to be tubbed, and scrubbed, and combed, and then put to bed, all red and shining, that the maids might go down-stairs to supper. And what with the combing, and the scrubbing, and the tubbing, the maids might be said to have fairly earned the best supper that could be provided for them. It was a terrific business. "Master Johnny, just you put down them snuffers, else I'll acquaint your pa." "Now, Freddy, wherever 'ave you laid the soap to? you've been and left it in the biling water, I do declare, till it's as white as that there counterpin, you good-for-nothing wasteful boy!" "And what are you two whispering about, I should like to know?" Such is a specimen of nurse's troubles on a Saturday evening about eight o'clock; and she was not generally left very long in doubt as to the subject on which Freddy and his brother were whispering. It was sure to be something of personal interest to herself. For the most part it would turn out to be some harmless practical joke, hurting nobody, and easily forgiven; but occasionally it became more serious, as, for instance,

2

when Johnny threw a cake of yellow soap at nurse's head, and smote her on the nose.

The first thing she did was to howl, and declare that she was dead: the next was to give palpable proof of being alive, by jumping up and vowing that she would go straight down-stairs and tell their father of them. Which also she did, leaving the boys in darkness.

"I say, we shall catch it," said Johnny. "We had better all pretend to be asleep."

"I sha'n't," said Freddy; "I shall put my trousers on."

The expediency of this measure was so obvious that it was adopted forthwith, and in less than two minutes the boys were all dressed again.

"I'm coming!" shouted a well-known voice on the stairs; and the boys, catching a certain whizzing sound in the distance, whispered one to another in fear and trembling, "He has got the spanker!" Now "the spanker" was a short and narrow piece of board, with a small hole at one end of it, which Parson Goggs had fashioned for the benefit of his offspring. He certainly had got the spanker, and he showed pretty evident signs of an intention to use it.

And then there was a scene. An uncommon one, let us hope, in most families; but common enough at Slappingham. The vicar was a pious man, and read his Bible; that is to say, he read little bits of it here and there with considerable diligence: and one of these little bits told him to beat his children's sides, so he beat them accordingly. There was another little bit somewhere, which told him to keep his temper; but he omitted to read that.

Little Johnny took his share of the spanker like a man, and then crawled into bed, and had out his cry under the sheets. Freddy was inclined to show fight, and persisted in catching hold of the weapon with his hand as it descended, whereupon his father gave him a double dose, and finally broke the spanker across his shoulders. There was nothing left, therefore, for Bobby but the palm of the paternal hand, which, however, was sufficiently well accustomed to its present work to take to it pretty kindly. The same hand had been writing an unctuous sermon not five minutes before, all about grace, and tenderness, and charity; but it was not on that account the less efficient in battering little Bobby's head; nor did it leave off its scriptural chastisement until it had caught the boy a foul blow on the face and made his nose bleed.

"I'll teach you to play tricks!" shouted the vicar, hissing at the child through his teeth. "Now, sir, go and wipe your face, and don't stand blubbering there." And he took a stride towards Bobby, as if he were going to hit him again; upon which the boy lost his balance, and fell off his bed with a heavy thump on the floor.

"Why does not he get up?" whispered one of the others. "Why does he lie there so still?"

"Because he is dead," said the other brother; "and I'll tell you something, Fred, if you will come closer. If the policeman finds it out, *papa will be hung!*"

"No, will he really?" said Freddy; not by way of disputing his elder brother's learning in such matters, but intimating that the subject was not so painful but

that he could endure to hear it discussed at greater
length.

But Bobby was not dead, nor anything near it.   He
was simply faint, and half stunned, and his affectionate
father might have brought him round in a couple of
minutes, if he had but known how.   Unfortunately,
however, he did not know how; and, for all the help
that he could give, Bobby might have lain there forever.   There he stood, pale and shivering with fright,
dangling the candle in his left hand, and spilling the
grease all over the floor, and looking like——well,
we won't say what he looked like.   To his own children, on such occasions, his visage was apt to suggest
comparisons more striking than complimentary.   "I
should like to know," they would say, "what old Bogie
can be like, if he is not like papa?"

"Bobby, my boy, are you hurt?" said the vicar,
at last, holding the candle down to the child's face.   It
was as pale as his own, and streaked with blood.   The
eyes were shut, the mouth half open, and the back of
the head jammed in between the wall and a projecting
knob of the iron bedstead.   It was not altogether a
pleasant sight for a father to look upon.

"Are you hurt, my boy?" he said again, whining
out the question as if he were the most affectionate of
parents.   He did not dare to touch him.   He was but
a clumsy sort of bully.   He had knocked his boy down,
but he had not the faintest notion how to pick him up
again.   This kind office therefore had to be performed
by the under-nurse, who had been washing the little
girls in the next room, and who now came to the rescue
with a mug of cold water.

"He'll be better directly," said Jemima Ann, taking up the boy in her strong fat arms, and laying him on the bed. And then the vicar slunk sheepishly out of the room, and went down to his sermon.

He was in the middle of a long quotation from "Romans," which neither he nor any one else could rightly understand, but upon which he intended nevertheless to dogmatize pretty strongly the next day, when the study door opened, and the mistress of the house came into the room. She had a shawl over her head, for she was an "invalid," and she found it necessary to protect herself against the chance of taking cold as she traveled from one room to another.

"What was that noise, my dear?" she asked, in a tone of voice which would have been intensely harsh and disagreeable had it not been so ridiculously feeble that you wondered how ever it got across the room.

"Only the boys romping up-stairs, love; there is nothing the matter."

"But I heard something fall, did I not?"

"Ah, that must have been Bobby. I believe he tripped up, and tumbled on the floor."

Now, if Parson Goggs had caught any of his children telling a fib, he would have proceeded on this wise. First, he would have asked the child half a dozen puzzling questions, so as to entrap him into telling a good many more lies than he had meant to tell. Secondly, he would have boxed his ears till he thought it scarcely safe to box them any more. Thirdly, he would have locked the boy up in a dark room by himself, to meditate upon his sin, visiting him at intervals of half an hour or so with alternate doses of tracts and hymns, and telling him, with many crocodile tears and solemn shakings of the head, what a depraved wretch he had shown himself to be; while the depraved wretch himself would suck his fingers in the corner, and wish his father and all his tracts and hymns at the bottom of the sea. For about a week afterwards the young sinner would have been in disgrace. His fault would have been brought up against him on all occasions, fitting or otherwise; and if he so much as joined in play with his brothers and sisters he would have been considered as hardened in his sin. Such was the righteous indignation of Parson Goggs when he heard a lie, and such his highly judicious mode of dealing with the liar.

Certainly, when the vicar's boys did tell lies—and I am afraid they told a good many—they made a better thing of it than their father did. Anybody could find him out, and his wife found him out directly. She knew by the very looks of him that he had been losing his temper; and she knew also to her cost that it was not such a very unusual thing. So she left him to his Bible, and went up-stairs to the nursery.

The children were all wide awake, and discussing in language not particularly respectful the temper and disposition of their papa. Mrs. Goggs, who always walked so softly that nobody could hear her coming, listened for a few minutes outside the door; but, as she had long ago discovered, by the same simple method, in what light she and her husband were regarded both by the servants and children, nothing that she heard on the present occasion struck her as particularly new or interesting. With a gentle sigh, therefore, partly no doubt at the wickedness of her boys, and partly because her trouble in listening had been so poorly repaid, she opened the door.

"You have quite made my head ache with your noise," she said. "Pray what were you all talking about so loudly as I came in?"

"Nothing, mamma, that I know of," said one of the boys at last.

"Nonsense, child; it must have been something. Come, sir, tell me immediately, or I shall fetch your papa." And she took up her candle again, as if she meant to go.

"It was Johnny, mamma," said Freddy, who, when he did tell a fib, made it a point of conscience to tell a good one. "He was saying his prayers out loud. He is always doing it."

"But there was some one else talking besides Johnny. I heard your voice, Freddy, I am sure."

"Oh, yes, mamma, I was telling him to be quiet, because Matthew vi. 8¹ tells us we ought to say our prayers to ourselves. Doesn't it, mamma?"

"You are all very naughty, wicked, sinful children, to tell such dreadful stories. Be silent, sir," she continued, seeing that Freddy was about to draw still further on his powers of invention. "I will not hear another word from you; and I will never, never, never believe you again. I know perfectly well what you were talking about, for I heard it on the stairs; and I shall tell your papa everything when I go down."

"Please not this time, mamma."

"Yes, I shall, Bobby; the very first thing on Monday morning—not to-night, lest the thought of your wickedness should disturb his mind through the blessed

Sabbath-day." After which cautious determination, and having satisfied herself that none of Bobby's bones were broken by his father's violence, Mrs. Goggs left the boys to themselves.

" Come and kiss me, mamma," said Freddy.

" No, Freddy, you are far too naughty to be kissed. I must see some decided change of heart in you before I can love you any more." Perhaps, on the whole, Freddy did not lose much. An embrace from such a woman might have given the poor child the nightmare. But though his mother would not salute him, he would on no account omit to salute his mother ; and this he did, as soon as her back was turned, after a fashion equally elegant and expressive.

If any one thinks this picture overdrawn, I suspect that it has not been his lot to meet many evangelical parsons, with invalid wives, large families, and somewhere about £400 a year.

About the time when he left the University and " went into the church," which I conceive to be the correct modern phrase for taking holy orders, young Goggs was by no means a bad sort of fellow. Without being either very clever or very wise, he had that happy knack of making himself generally agreeable, which is a talent in itself ; and while serving his first curacy at a proprietary chapel in London, he contrived to make himself so especially agreeable to Miss Elizabeth Ague, a young lady who rented a thirty-shilling seat in the gallery, that she provided him with bands and slippers for three calendar months, and then committed herself and all her worldly goods into his charge. The first item in this important trust consisted of a plain mealy

face, with very regular lady-like features, and no ex-
pression at all. The second was a sum of £2000 in
the funds, bequeathed to her by a pious aunt, on condition that she attended three Bible Society meetings
every year, collected half a crown a quarter in penny
subscriptions for the missionaries, and never married
any one whose views were not in accordance with 2
Timothy iii. 19. There could be no doubt whatever
about Mr. Goggs's views, so she married him; and he
was soon afterwards presented by Simeon's trustees to
the vicarage of Slappingham, in the diocese of Dumplington.

Here he found out, after a very short experience,
that Miss Ague was not precisely the wife to make a
parson happy. She had always, according to her own
account, "enjoyed" bad health; and she now became
so absurdly nervous and hypochondriacal as to settle
down at last into that most selfish and most useless of
beings, an invalid. And sorely did her husband regret
the day when she and her £2000 came into his possession. For the incessant whining of his partner's lan-
guid voice—the nuisance of living in a house where
not a door might be left open for fear of the draught,
or banged for fear of upsetting the mistress's nerves;
not to mention the difficulty of paying the butcher's
bill, and of providing medicine enough, at eighteen-
pence the bottle, to satisfy the imaginary cravings of
Mrs. Goggs's exhausted system: these things had so
worried and soured the vicar's temper that any old
college friend would scarcely have known him. And
they had done worse than sour his temper. They had
made him a hypocrite and a humbug. Poverty had

taught him all kinds of mean shifts for making ends meet. As his quiver became full, his perceptions of what was generous and upright grew less and less keen. Stingy contrivances which would once have seemed to him intolerable had now to be tolerated every day; and though at first he could not help being disgusted at his wife's meanness, he gradually became reconciled to her doctrine that in the cause of domestic economy anything is lawful. And the principal sufferers from the code of household laws thus framed were of course the children. Servants will not be "put upon" in the matter of beef and mutton. When supplies fail, they can give notice and go. But the poor children had no such remedy; so they munched their stale bread and drank their lukewarm milk-and-water, looking forward to glorious days when they should be grown up, and should never touch bread any more, but should devour huge slices of cake, spread an inch thick with jam and clotted cream. Meanwhile they were not without some privileges, for occasionally it was permitted to them to come down-stairs to breakfast, and to watch their parents eating kidneys and broiled ham. And sometimes, if an egg were sent in which would have been very nice and fresh a few days before, the vicar would generously make over the savory morsel to one of his boys. "Bobby has been a good boy lately," he would say, making a horrible face as he broke the shell, "and he shall have my egg, for a great treat. And, Bobby, you had better go and eat it in the kitchen, for fear you should dirty the clean cloth;" the cloth having been washed, as Bobby and his father both knew well enough, something like three weeks ago. Such were some of the instructive lessons which the Slappingham children learned from their papa and mamma. And if these lessons were remembered and acted upon in after-life, we can scarcely be surprised.

When Mrs. Goggs left the nursery she rejoined her husband in the study, and sat mending Bobby's socks until ten o'clock. About this time a tray was brought in, and the vicar, having finished the peroration of his sermon, mixed himself a tumbler of something and water, and handed a wineglassful of the same compound to his wife. Which comforting beverage having been sipped in silence, the pious couple retired to rest.

CHAPTER III.

MR. GOGGS CONVERSES WITH A REVEREND BROTHER.

THE next morning Bobby woke up with a headache, and a feverish pulse. "I don't mean to lie in bed, though," said Bobby to the nurse, "or else I shall have to take a horrid dose of rhubarb and magnesia, or castor oil." There was a considerable amount of nasty medicine consumed in the Slappingham nursery in the course of a year. The air was dry and bracing, and the children's appetites enormous; so enormous that an occasional pill or powder was found to be a convenient and economical check upon them. It was not very probable that Bobby would escape the infliction; and his father settled the question for him by visiting him in his dressing-gown.

"Well, my precious boy, how are you this bright Sabbath morning? You know the hymn, do you not? 'Awake, my soul, and with the sun'——"

"Yes, papa, 'Improve each shining hour.'" But Bobby was not permitted to finish the verse, for his affectionate father hit him a blow on the cheek which left its red mark for an hour or more.

"Oh, papa!" cried Bobby, shrinking away into the farthest corner of his little bed.

"I'll teach you to make fun of the Hymn Book, sir, that I will."

"But I thought that was right, papa, really. Only I have such a lot of things to learn I can't remember them all."

"Don't tell me any more lies, sir, but put out your tongue directly."

This was not so very easy, considering that the poor child was shaking with his sobs. He did, however, manage to get his tongue out at last, though that unfortunate member got terribly bitten in the process.

"There is nothing the matter with the boy," said the vicar; "only a bilious attack. You have been eating and drinking too much, sir, that is what it is."

Poor Bobby! it was little enough, in the way of nice unwholesome things, that he had to eat and drink. He scarcely knew the taste of anything but dry bread, boiled rice, and cold mutton. But every ailment at Slappingham was set down as a bilious attack, so Bobby swallowed his nauseous poison like a man, not even daring to make a face as he gave the glass back to his father. And then the vicar went down to shave—let us hope successfully. Let us hope that he did not, in a careless moment, inflict a wound upon his reverend chin. Let us hope, if he did chance to do so, that he employed no ejaculation unbecoming in a clergyman. Let us hope, moreover, supposing that he had gashed himself pretty severely, that his dear children would have been properly grieved.

I believe that I should be thought an unnatural monster if I were to say that Bobby and his brothers and sisters hated the very sight of their father and mother. But why they should be supposed to love them is more than I could tell. They had scarcely ever received from them a really kind word. Now and then there was some pretense of affection, when the vicar would put on a silly, playful manner, which did not become him in the least, and in a whining, sentimental voice would call one of them his own precious child, and quote a text of Scripture at him. But the precious child took all that for what it was worth, knowing that his father was as likely as not to fly into a passion the next minute, and box his ears. And yet, strange to say, Parson Goggs thought himself the very model of an affectionate parent. He believed that no one in the world understood the art of bringing up children as well as he did. His discipline was so admirable, his boys so perfectly under command ; their religious tone so high—their acquaintance with the Bible so exten-sive—their observations so intelligent—their innocence of the ways of the world so refreshing. The foolish man did not consider how dearly he paid for having his children under command, seeing that he had made them afraid of the very sound of his footstep, and de-stroyed forever all chance of gaining their confidence. It never occurred to him to ask whether either they or he understood the meaning of half the texts which were always at their tongues' end, apropos of nothing at all; nor did he for a moment suspect that their religious talk and precocious questions were all put on for a pur-pose, because the little rogues were sharp enough to see how to get the right side of their evangelical papa. And as for their innocence of the ways of the world, the parson forgot that there are worse ways than these ; and that when children are taught deceit both by pre-cept and example, and encouraged by various means to become dishonest little humbugs, they are pretty sure to find out for themselves the very worst ways that a child can possibly follow.

When the vicar came into the breakfast-room at eight o'clock to read prayers, the postman was passing the window with the vicarage letter-bag hanging behind his back. But he was not allowed to leave the bag on a Sunday, so he trudged on to the post-office in the village. Parson Goggs was a rigid observer of the Sabbath-day—at least, he meant to be—only, poor man, he was always just a day too late, mistaking Sunday for Saturday. He would not have written a letter, or opened one, on a Sunday, for any consideration. "What are you reading, Bobby?" he would ask, on a Sunday evening after tea. "Pilgrim's Progress, papa." "Then put it away, my boy. The Bible on Sunday, and the Bible only." Which wise regulation did not, I suspect, increase Master Bobby's love either for the Bible or the Sabbath-day.

So the postman tramped on ; and at five o'clock in the evening he tramped backed again, having left the parson's letters at the village post-office; and the letters were brought to the vicarage on Monday morning by a small village maiden. It was on Monday morning, then, that the vicar found out what an important letter he had missed. "Rev. Sir" (said the letter), "Mr. Barroll is dangerously ill, and wishes to see yourself or Mrs. Goggs immediately. Your obedient servant, John Jones."

Now, Mr. Barroll was Parson Goggs's uncle, who had lately retired from the well-known and highly-respectable house of Barroll & Corke, brewers, and

was supposed to be worth about forty thousand pounds.
He had quarreled with his nephew many years ago,
ever since the parson had had the bad taste to throw in
his teeth that he was a brewer, and lived on the drunk-
enness of the multitude.   Then and there did the old
gentleman vow that his relative should never touch a
sixpence of his ill-gotten wealth, and he had hitherto
most religiously kept his word.   But when the doctor
told him that he was going to die, he thought better of
it, and made his lawyer write off at once for Parson
Goggs.

"Is he not come?" asked the sick man, about the
middle of the day on Sunday.

"No, sir," said the doctor.   "It is Sunday, you
know.   Perhaps he could not get his duty done."

"That would not prevent his wife from coming,
would it, stupid?" growled the brewer, who had no
respect for doctors even in the hour of his dissolu-
tion.

"Ah, he won't see me," muttered the old man at
last.   "He won't defile himself with the dirty money.
Then it shall go as I have left it, to Harry Northcote.
If he had come he should have had the half of it for
his trouble."

Harry Northcote was the only child of a navy captain on half pay, who rented a small cottage on Mr.
Barroll's estate, and was distantly related to the
brewer.   As the captain was the finest old fellow living, and his child the very dearest boy that ever was
born, the Squire had seen a good deal of them, though
no one ever dreamed that he would make either of
them his heir.   Indeed, it was generally understood

that he had left his money among some half dozen societies, religious or otherwise. Now, however, Harry Northcote was to have it all; and when the old man had settled in his mind that the will should stand, he lingered yet a few more hours and died, just as Parson Goggs was reading for the twenty-fifth time his unfortunate letter and pondering deeply within himself what he could possibly do.

"But you know, my dear," whined Mrs. Goggs, consolingly, "if you had got the letter yesterday you could not have gone. Think of Divine service."

"That would have been easily managed, my love. Sims would have sent his curate over from Clayton, and he is quite a right-minded young man, and an admirable expounder, as far as his light goes."

"Does he preach the *whole* truth, papa?" asked Bobby; for Bobby was out of disgrace now, and was anxious to keep on good terms with his father.

The Parson looked hard at his son for a moment, as if he were doubtful whether it were a hoax or not; but Bobby kept his countenance beautifully. "Precious boy," said his father at last, gently shaking his head, and smiling with watery eyes at his first-born. "Come and kiss me, dear." So Bobby went round the table to be kissed, and brought back with him by way of a more substantial reward a piece of bacon off his father's plate, which indeed his father could well spare, seeing that it had become perfectly cold during the reading of the letter. But Bobby had not quite played out his little game yet, for he sneaked up to his mother also, who stroked his hair and kissed him and filled up his

mug of milk and water with some nice hot tea. A
sharp boy was Master Bobby.

And then Bobby was dismissed, and a solemn consultation was held in the breakfast-room as to the best
plan to be adopted. It was but six miles to Dumplington, the county town. Why should not the Parson
get a lift in Farmer Swede's cart, and catch the afternoon train for Aleworth, where his uncle lived? Or
else, better still, there was the Rev. Ebenezer Slimes,
Baptist minister from Dumplington, who, in compas-
sion to the benighted souls at Slappingham, drove into
the village every Saturday evening, and out again on
Monday. The red brick parallelogram in which he
held forth on Sunday was crammed to suffocation,
for he was pious and painful, and his vernacular unex-
ceptionable. "You bees all a going to wrath together,"
was his warning to sinners who were irregular in their
attendance or meager in their offerings. "You be
straight on the road to glory," was his encouragement
to the saints who rewarded his disinterested labors by
inviting him to dine. A drive of six miles with such
a man must be a spiritual benefit, if not an intellectual
treat, to the Vicar of Slappingham. What if they differed in some unimportant points here and there?
What if Mr. Slimes thought the three creeds a fiction,
and the Prayer Book a device of the enemy? At least
they had something in common. They both agreed
that the Pope was Antichrist, and Puseyism rank idol-
atry. This bond of union was surely of sufficient
strength to keep them together for six miles. And
what an example of brotherly love to the parish all

around to see the Clergyman and the Methody driven along side by side !   .

Mr. Slimes was only too happy. It would be the proudest moment of his life to be of any assistance to a brother minister. A drop of something warm before starting? Certainly he would not object. It was his duty to his flock to keep out the cold. Another drop? Well, really, if he might but have a sandwich with it he thought he could manage to take it down. And so at last they started ; Mrs. Goggs, watching their departure from the front door, not without some apprehension as to the fate of her flower borders, and congratulating herself that the vicarage gate, if they should drive up against it, was tolerably firm on its hinges.

Decency demands that a veil should be drawn over the conversation which then ensued. There are some subjects too solemn to be played with ; and the levity, the coarse flippant impudence, with which our two friends handled sacred things, may not be characterized in these pages, even to point a moral or adorn a tale. One has heard drunkards blaspheme and madmen rave ; but for downright cool profanity, for simple prostitution of all that men and angels reverence, give me a couple of Evangelical ministers talking Scripture during a six-mile drive.

They had just disposed, to their intense satisfaction, of one of the most abstruse mysteries of the Christian faith, when the cart rattled under an archway, and round a sharp corner, and brought the grand old towers of Dumplington Cathedral into view. It was instructive to contrast the conduct of the two men. The one

who had lived in the ancient city all his life, and to
whom the very sight of a gable or a turret was an eye-
sore, would scarcely turn his head to behold so glaring
a relic of Popish days; while the other, resident six
miles off, but not without hope that some pleasant
cathedral appointment might one day bring him nearer,
gazed with equal interest and admiration at the noble
group of buildings before him.   The two great towers,
stern and heavy as if they meant to stand forever, and
yet relieved in their awful grandeur by countless alter-
nations of light and shade ; the pinnacles, their golden
crests flashing in the sunlight, as if some bright bird of
heaven had perched upon them, and was clapping his
wings for joy ; the buttresses, standing out like giant
watchmen, to guard the hallowed walls ; the outline, so
crisp and sharp, and yet so wondrously irregular, losing
itself in the intricacy of its wanderings, yet ever point-
ing its clear mark against the sky, as though the majesty
of the art would preach to us, with our ill-defined principles and our narrow minds, "I will go hither and
thither just where I please, but wherever I do go I will
show a line."   And, indeed, whether for art or higher
things than art, what preacher half so eloquent ? what
witness half so uncompromising to the churchmanship
of our English faith?   You may argue with lovers of
argument as fiercely as you please, but take one glance
at your cathedral tower and the whole question of High
Church or Low Church is settled for you.   What does
the building mean ?   Has it any sense whatever, except
on the admission that worship is to be rich and beautiful, and not poor and cold?

"And where does your reverence intend to bide?" asked Mr. Slimes, paying a graceful, and, doubtless, a highly gratifying tribute to the validity of his rival's ministerial call.

"I generally stop at the Red Lion; and as I may have to wait nearly an hour for the train, perhaps I had better go there now."

"Expensive 'ouse, sir; expensive 'ouse, werry. Charge you two shillings for a scrap of stewed steak, and don't put no onions round."

"Don't they, really?"

"No, sir, they don't. Now, I knows of a 'ouse, 'ighly respectable 'ouse, too, where you gets a plate of good 'olesome meat and a tatur for sixpence, stand and eat it at the bar; and an ordinary every Tuesday and Friday for one and nine."

"Do you, indeed?"

"Fact, sir. It's the Peacock, in Slipper Lane, that is the name of it, sir. And as I happen to be going there myself, I shall be proud to drive you there. Only say you are a friend of mine, and they will serve you for nothing a'most. The 'ouse is kept by my wife's cousin."

Ill-natured people did say that Mr. Slimes's wife's cousin aforesaid might, with more strict adherence to truth, have been described as his wife's husband. Certain it is that the Peacock in Slipper Lane had served the pious preacher for a residence during a long term of years, in the course of which—so the common report declared—he had combined, with considerable advantage to himself, the offices of publican and pharisee.

There was but little doing in Dumplington on a Sunday; and, for a family man with a serious turn, a preachment in the country proved a healthy and lucrative employment of the day. Extremes meet, all the world over; Friar Tuck himself was no better than a bandit; and doubtless our friend's eloquence in the pulpit was not the less impressive because of the refined character and choice languages of his associates as he plied his weekday trade.

CHAPTER IV.

MR. GOGGS RESOLVES TO KEEP A SCHOOL.

To be regaled at the Peacock, off good wholesome meat and potatoes, for nothing a'most, was a chance not to be lost, and Parson Goggs readily availed himself of his companion's kind offer. On driving into the yard, Mr. Slimes made over the horse and cart to the care of the hostler, and, shaking hands with his reverend brother, disappeared among the intricate passages of the hostelry,—intent, probably, on the task of reporting his arrival to his wife's cousin. The vicar meanwhile found his way to the commercial room—a dingy-looking apartment, furnished with the usual number of horsehair chairs, and fragrant with the ordinary scent of stale tobacco.

The waiter who answered his bell ushered into the room at the same moment a tall solemn-looking gentleman, dressed entirely in black, with a hat almost covered with crape, and a crumpled white necktie. "The *black* horse, if you please, James," said the solemn gentleman ; "and the *black* four-wheel."

"Very sorry, sir," replied the waiter, "but they are both out. Seed 'em go early this morning. There's none of 'em at home, sir, except it's the chestnut mare with white stockings."

"James," said the solemn gentleman, reproachfully, "it is quite impossible. You forget that my journey to-day will be a painful one—a very painful one indeed. How could I ever drive up to the door of our lamented friend behind a chestnut mare with white stockings?"

"Then I'll be blowed if there's e'er another," answered James, rather tired of the conversation. "What for *you*, sir, please?" he continued affably, turning to Mr. Goggs, who was studying a county map upon the wall.

"I was wanting some luncheon," observed Mr. Goggs. "My friend Mr. Slimes mentioned——"

"Yes, sir; did you wish to see the governor, sir? He's in the parlor, along with missis. Oh, I ask your pardon, sir. You're the gent as has just a driven in with master from the country. Luncheon, sir? Yes, sir, what would you please to take, sir? There's cold roast beef, cold boiled beef, cold ham, ch——"

"Now don't, my friend," interrupted Mr. Goggs, smiling facetiously, "pray don't go on. I know what you are going to say. Of course I can have chops or steaks. But isn't there anything a little more out of the common? A nice slice of roast mutton, now, and a baked potato?"

"I'll inquire, sir," said the waiter, not very well pleased at having his bill of fare taken out of his mouth, and proceeding to lay the cloth for one, in anticipation of the forthcoming food.

"I must have the chestnut mare, James," sighed the solemn gentleman, as the waiter left the room, after putting upon the table a cruet-stand with two legs, a two-edged knife, a fork with the electro-plate very much worn away, a slab of stale bread, and a vessel peculiar to commercial inns and refreshment-rooms, which looked like a wineglass blown several sizes too big, and turned into a tumbler.

"Very good, sir," replied James, grinning. "I'll tell somebody in the yard to bring her round."

"I fear, sir," began Mr. Goggs, wishing to be civil to the solemn gentleman, "I fear that by the dispensation of Providence you are lamenting the loss of some near relation."

"A very dear and valued friend, sir," said the solemn gentleman, with a bow, "but no relation. It was impossible, sir, to know such a man as the late Mr. Barroll, and not to shed tears of unfeigned sorrow at his loss!" And here the solemn gentleman drew a handkerchief from his pocket, ready to catch the tears of unfeigned sorrow, in case by any accident they should fall.

"Is my poor uncle dead?" ejaculated Mr. Goggs. "Oh, dear, dear, dear! then I am too late, after all!"

"It would appear so, sir; though I was not aware that I had the honor of addressing a relative of the deceased. You are going over to Aleworth, I presume, sir, by the two o'clock train?"

"Such was my purpose, D.V.," replied Mr. Goggs, providing with pious reservation for all possible contingencies.

"Might I be permitted, sir, the melancholy pleasure of driving you over? I shall be starting almost immediately,—as soon as you have finished your mutton and baked potatoes. We shall reach the domain of my lamented friend and your revered uncle quite as soon as the train; and I shall enjoy—ar—the privilege of your—ar—company."

This was an offer not to be refused; and Mr. Goggs accepted it forthwith. In less than twenty minutes he was sitting beside the solemn gentleman in a rickety brown cart, drawn at the rate of six miles an hour by the chestnut mare with white stockings.

The Vicar of Slappingham could not think what on earth the solemn gentleman wanted at Aleworth. He was not a doctor; certainly not a parson. Who could he possibly be?

"Shall you stay long at the house?" he ventured to ask at length, when the chestnut mare with white stockings had trotted a mile or two on the road.

"Back to-night, sir," said the solemn gentleman, "as soon as I have taken the requisite dimensions."

"Requisite dimensions!" repeated his companion. "What can you possibly mean?" Surely they were not going to paper the rooms afresh, when his uncle's body was scarcely cold.

"Oh, sir," explained the solemn gentleman, with increased solemnity, "it is our mournful duty, in the profession to which I belong, to measure the deceased for the tabernacles which must enshrine their mortal remains." And, as he spoke, he shifted the reins to his left hand, and drew a roll of tape from his pocket, looking all the while at the vicar as if it would afford him unmingled satisfaction to lay him out, and take his measure for a tabernacle, then and there.

"Good gracious!" said Mr. Goggs, shrinking away from his new friend till he nearly tumbled out of the cart, "then you are the under——"

"Just so, sir," replied the solemn gentleman, "the undertaker. But," he added, mercifully smiling as if to reassure his fellow-traveler, "we have duties to the living, sir, as well as to the dead; and if at any time you should be furnishing, or removing goods by rail, we shall be proud to accommodate you, at a reasonable charge."

"You are very kind," said Mr. Goggs, who fidgeted on his seat, and spoke in monosyllables for the rest of the journey. It was not very pleasant to sit for a drive of ten miles beside a man who was going to measure your uncle for a coffin; and our poor vicar felt extremely like a corpse as the practiced eye of the undertaker seemed ever and again to turn upon him, and to calculate approximately how many feet he would occupy in the clear.

However, the drive came to an end at last. The solemn gentleman took his measurements and entered his instructions in a little black-edged book, and the chestnut mare with white stockings bore him safely home; while Mr. Goggs, as was natural and decent, remained at his uncle's house until the funeral was over, and the distribution of the forty thousand pounds had been made known.

Then he too went back to Dumplington; not a blighted man, inasmuch as he had really expected nothing; but certainly a disappointed man, and most undoubtedly an injured man. His uncle's will was cruel and unjust; but we must do our vicar the credit to declare, that he of all men in the world was probably the least disposed to quarrel with it. A legacy would have been very acceptable, for his children's sake as

well as for his own; but he had not reckoned upon it,
and he could pay his bills without it. Certainly, it
was hard to have been expressly summoned, and made
to act the part of chief mourner, and then to sit in
the library, and find himself passed over, and hear
others named as legatees. Certainly, the Vicar of
Slappingham, as he took his second-class ticket at the
station on his journey home, felt no consuming love
for Harry Northcote, the inheritor of his uncle's
wealth. And certainly, when he remembered what
the doctor had said to him at Aleworth, that half
the brewer's hoard must surely have been his, but for
that confounded Sunday postman, the father of a family got the better of the evangelical minister, and some
very naughty words were muttered between the pious
parson's teeth—words so naughty that, when he muttered them again in his sleep at night, Mrs. Goggs
arose in terror from his side, and read him, in her
cold sepulchral voice, so many chapters from the
Revelations of Dr. Cumming, that never, sleeping or
waking, did the poor man venture to forget himself
again.

On his way through Dumplington the vicar halted
again at the Peacock in Slipper Lane, and refreshed
himself with another slice of mutton and a baked
potato. During his meal he read the Dumplington
Gazette, in the columns of which a conspicuous adver-
tisement caught his eye.

SCHOLASTIC.—The Trustees of the Dumplington
Grammar-School require the services of a compe-
tent Head-Master immediately. Salary £500 a year,

with a house for boarders. Must be a clergyman of
the Established Church. No Ritualist need apply.
Testimonials to be sent to Peter Teasel, Esq., Clerk to
the Trustees.

"The very thing for me!" said the vicar to himself. "I'll see the bishop about it this very afternoon."

The bishop gave our friend an excellent testimonial,
the dean gave him another, and half a dozen influen-
tial residents in Dumplington promised him all the
assistance in their power. "I was made for a schoolmaster, my lord," said Mr. Goggs, thinking of the
spanker; "and I am sure my dear wife will be a pat-
tern of motherly kindness to the boys."

"I am sure she will," said the bishop, who had
never seen the lady in his life; "and I wish you, my
dear friend, every possible success. If you will take
my advice, you will call on Mr. Teasel, and let him
know at once that you mean to stand."

Mr. Teasel's office was in the Close, somewhat to
the disgust of the accredited ecclesiastical lawyer of
Dumplington. But his business was purely, or im-
purely, secular. Nobody knew exactly what he did,
except that he made money all the week, and reckoned
up his gains in church on Sunday. The parson thought
sometimes that he was taking notes of his sermon; but
Mr. Teasel's neighbors knew better. His Prayer Book
was covered with figures in every page; and he had
been known, in fits of abstraction, to make mysterious
calculations in the lining of his fellow-worshiper's
hat. He was at home when Mr. Goggs called upon
him; and he gave the reverend gentleman every en-

couragement to persevere in his canvass for the Head-
Mastership of the Grammar-School.

"You are the first in the field, Mr. Goggs," said
the lawyer, "and I should think, speaking with cau-
tion, that your principles would suit the trustees. They
are all Dissenters, you know, every man alive of them;
and they would put in Greasie, the Baptist minister,
in a moment, if the statutes would let them. But I
really believe that, next to Greasie, they would like
best to have you."

Mr. Goggs was just acknowledging in suitable terms
this most gratifying compliment, when the door of the
office flew open, and two young ladies, each ornamented with a head of bright red hair, raced each
other into the room. "Oh, papa!" they both cried
at once, far too excited to be abashed by the presence
of a stranger, "have you heard the news? What *do*
you think? The old Earl of Appletree has gone and
married his cook!"

CHAPTER V.

SHOWING HOW THE EARL CAME TO DO IT.

IT was a silly thing to do. There could be no doubt whatever about that. He might have had almost any one else he pleased. Half the girls in the county would have trotted along with the dear old man to the nearest parish church, and married him at ten minutes' notice, any day or any night, license or no license, banns or no banns, and even, if decency had not forbidden it, parson or no parson. But he would not ask any one of them; and so he lived a bachelor till he was sixty-five, and then—married his cook.

It was a shabby thing to do. There could be no doubt about that either. Here was young Tom Pippin, the best fellow in the world, but, like many other best fellows, as poor as a rat; Tom Pippin, whom everybody liked; who was the best company, the best shot, the best rider, the best cricketer, and the best billiard-player for a hundred miles round; Tom Pippin, who was up to his ears in love with the prettiest girl that ever was seen, but did not dare talk of marrying her till his uncle was——no, till the title and property came to him, as he thought that some day they probably might; here was Tom Pippin with all his brilliant prospects clouded over, and his glorious expectation

of enormous wealth and high position reduced to the
faint glimmering of a hope, first, that his dear little
cousin might never arrive at all; secondly, that if it
did arrive, it might be—any species of living creature
you please except a boy; thirdly, that if it were a
boy it might be spared the misery of cutting its little
teeth, by cutting its little lucky on the earliest convenient occasion.

But it was something worse than either of these.   It
was a nasty thing to do.   People do silly things every
day, and shabby things every day, and somehow or
other they get forgiven; but no one will forgive a man,
still less a woman, who does a nasty thing.   If the old
earl *must* marry a servant, why could not he have taken
little Polly Sanders, the black-eyed maiden at the
Model Farm; or even Betty Stokes, the park-keeper's
daughter at the lodge?   But a horrid, fat——ugh!
what a taste old men must have, to be sure!

She was not even a decently good cook.   If she had
been, one might have supposed that her master was
taken captive by her soft allurements in the region
where some men are so susceptible.   But the dinners
down at Crab Cottage, the little country place where
the earl lived for about six weeks every year, and
where he picked up his bride, were never so well
dressed as to set any one in love with the goddess of
the kitchen.   Mutton must be very tender and very
well served, if it is to feed the affections as well as
satisfy the cravings of hunger.   Birds must indeed be
roasted to a turn, ere a man will long to clasp in
matrimony the hand that basted them; and bread
sauce be something more than perfect, which can make

one pine to rest one's head upon the bosom that has
throbbed with anxiety lest it should stay in the pot too
long.   Possibly Lord Appletree was so keenly alive to
his want of a new cook that any means seemed plausible which might rid him of the old one.

Married, however, they certainly were ; and when,
three or four months after the wedding, the gentlemen
of the county had expended their indignation in
abusing the old man for throwing himself so hopelessly
away, the ladies of the county began to take the matter up from their own peculiar point of view, and to
whisper prettily among themselves about another little
event, which seemed likely in due time to make a sensation in their small world.

At last the little event came ; and, to the intense
disgust of poor Tom Pippin, it turned out to be neither
a prehistoric curiosity, nor an undiscovered species,
nor even a girl, but a great fat hearty boy, born, as the
nurse declared, with a regular head of hair, and crow-
ing like a little game-cock almost before she could get
him into her arms.   Here was a pretty sort of a young
viscount to inherit all the glories of Dumplingshire !
Half the acres in the county belonged to the earl ;
and now they would all go to a wretched little brat
whose mother no doctor's or parson's wife could possibly receive.   It was enough to make any one turn
republican.   Landed proprietors and noble families
were all very well ; but, if the aristocracy played such
tricks as this, we had better be without them ; better
cut up their estates into allotments, and let us all start
fair, each man upon his little plot of ground. So thought
the Dumplingshire folk, disgusted with the old earl's

unpresentable wife; disgusted with his plebeian heir; and disgusted perhaps most of all with the prospect of a long minority, during which the great house at Withycombe would be empty, and the whole neighborhood dull, while an already fabulous income was doubling itself for the benefit of the cook's boy.

The earl, however, was beside himself with delight. He was a little man, and a hideously ugly little man, with a pug nose, and great thick lips, and red eyes, one of which did not point quite true. Why noble earls should so often be ugly, is a problem in nature, seeing that their fathers and grandfathers for generations past must have had the pick of all the pretty women in the kingdom. But certain it is that, for one really good-looking aristocrat, you meet with half a dozen whose appearance is, to say the least, so absolutely commonplace, that if you did not see all the world making way for them, hat in hand, you would scarcely suppose them to be gentlemen. Such a one was Lord Appletree. In his best days he might have driven an omnibus without seeming one bit above his work; and, now that he was old and wrinkled, you would have thought it the most natural thing in the world if he had accosted you at the corner of Farringdon Street with a broom.

How the old fellow chuckled when he heard the good news! He was in town when it reached him, at his little bachelor establishment in Bolton Street, May Fair; where perhaps he was leading somewhat more of a bachelor life than his buxom countess might have approved. But he vowed eternal gratitude to the wife who had been so good to him; and sent her down all

the presents he could think of, by way of consolation
for his own absence at so interesting a time. And, as
soon as ever his bachelor engagements were fulfilled,
he put himself in the train, and hurried down to Withycombe, to superintend in person the necessary festivities at the christening of his son and heir.

It was some disappointment to the old man, as he
drew near home, to see how little enthusiasm the great
event had aroused. Dumplington, the capital of his own
county, was just as quiet and just as fast asleep as if this
lucky young heir to one hundred thousand pounds a
year had never been born. To be sure, Dumplington was a Cathedral town, but the earl knew very well
that even the Close itself would have shaken off dull
sloth and hung out flags to welcome his boy, if his boy's
mother had not been a cook. So he shook his fist at
the old Norman towers, and swore between his teeth
at the bigotry of the parsons and the prejudice of the
world, and had himself driven from the station out to
Withycombe House, without a hat waved in his honor,
and without a cheer. Let us hope that the smiles of
his lady made it up to him when he reached home.

Lady Appletree was a sensible woman, who obsti-
nately refused to eat gruel and broth, merely because
the doctor told her that the functions of her ladyship's
system were temporarily deranged. "Stuff and nonsense, doctor!" said she; "I'll trouble you for a
mutton-chop and some porter. Deranged, indeed!
Just like your impudence. You go and starve a poor
body, and then tell her that she is deranged!" The
consequence was that in less than a fortnight the
buxom countess was down-stairs again, dining with

her noble husband at seven o'clock, and eagerly discussing plans for the forthcoming festivities.

The question of sponsors had been rather a difficult one to settle. The noble relatives of the great house of Pippin were much too angry to have anything to do with it; and the earl really began to think that he must call in the assistance of the parish clerk. At last he prevailed upon Sir John Montgomery, a poor Scotch baronet, whom at sundry times his lordship had decidedly snubbed for his poverty, to do the kind office for his son and heir. The Dumplington doctor, who was also a Scotchman, and a man of decently good family, consented to stand by the baronet's side; and his sister, an ancient maiden, who lived with him and kept house, completed the number. The boy was to be called Horatio Adolphus Plantagenet Leicester Montgomery Stuart; half a dozen names being the smallest number to which the eldest son of an earl could condescend. There was to be a big dinner on Monday, a performance of private theatricals on Tuesday, and a ball on Wednesday. The rest of the week was to be given up to the entertainment of the tenants and their wives and families, and every laborer on the estate was to be provided with the means of making merry. The whole thing was to be done in style; and all the county should see that Lord Appletree was not one bit ashamed of having married his cook. If the great people did not choose to come, let them stay away, and the house should be filled with little people instead. Not that the earl had much fear about that. He had not lived sixty-five years in this funny world without learning something about its funny ways. He knew very well that all the stuck-up squires, who now made believe to cut him, because he had married his cook, would come running up to him like little dogs, as soon as he chose to whistle for them. He knew that the bishop, who had politely declined to christen his boy, and the country parsons who had followed their diocesan's apostolical lead, would come and kneel in a row before him, the moment they wanted to ask a favor. This was Lord Appletree's philosophy; and he felt that he could afford to laugh, as he saw nose after nose in Dumplingshire turned up at his countess-cook.

In due course, the great week arrived; and the little baby lord was baptized in Withycombe church on the Sunday afternoon, in the presence of a large congregation, including the select family party assembled for the occasion at the great house. This party was very select, indeed, being a party of five, besides the countess and the earl.

Tom Pippin was there, cursing his ill luck, but not daring to offend his uncle by refusing to come. Dr. Stuart was there, and Miss Stuart, and Sir John Montgomery and Miss Montgomery. Now Miss Montgomery was the very identical prettiest girl that ever was seen, with whom Tom Pippin was up to his ears in love.

And no wonder. She was intensely beautiful, and as good as gold. Beautiful girls are common enough, each one beautiful in her own especial style, beautiful in spite of some abominably bad taste in dress, or some hideous deformity in the arrangement of her hair. There is the sparkling beauty, and the wicked beauty, and the sleepy languishing beauty, and the shrinking modest beauty, and the cold marble beauty, and the thick-lipped short-faced winning beauty, which to most men is simply irresistible. All these are very well for a romp, or a picnic, or a flirtation, or a dance, or to take down to dinner. But, when you come to talk of marrying, there are better things than beauty after all —things beside which the various types of loveliness are scarcely worth comparing. Your Phyllis may be a heartless coquette, and you will write ditties to her still; but your wife must be a woman and a lady. They are not so very common, either of them. A perfect lady; nice in all her tastes and all her belongings; with everything about her thoroughly nice, from the crown of her head to the sole of her foot; so nice that nothing of hers need at any time be concealed, but all will bear looking into with ever so fastidious an eye. Of many pretty young ladies of the present day it must needs be said that they are by no means nice; that there are things about them which will not bear looking into at all; that their laundress scarcely divides her fair share of profits with the dressmaker; and that it would be well if half the time spent each morning in the elaborate disfigurement of the back of their heads had been employed—must I say it?—in the refreshing application of soap and water. A slovenly man is bad enough; but a slovenly woman is something too awful to be endured.

And she must be very, very good; good-natured, generous and kind; good-hearted, loving, and true; good-tempered, unsuspicious, and trustful. She must be good in a higher sense still; pure and guileless, and

fearing God; and if you can find such a woman, never
mind about her eyelashes, or the chiseling of her nose,
but go in and win her, and and you will have a wife
indeed.

Such a woman was Edith Montgomery; and it will
be readily believed, by those who know what the affections of most young men are worth, that she was by
many degrees too good for Tom Pippin. It is not of
much use to try and describe him. Those who care to
know what he was like may go into a club, or walk
down Pall Mall, or join any group of well-dressed,
good-looking, empty-headed gentlemen of between
twenty and thirty years of age, and any one of them
will do for Tom Pippin. In some respects, indeed, he
was better than most, inasmuch as he really did excel
in divers rural sports and manly games. He was wonderfully handsome, and very active and strong; and he
had turned his natural gifts to so good an account as to
be one of the best sportsmen and one of the greatest
athletes in his county. But in all other matters he
was simply a fool; and his conversation, whether with
man or woman, began with "By Jove" and ended
with "haw, haw." For a short time he had held a
commission in the army; but after his father's death
he sold out, and lived as best he might upon the expectation of succeeding to his uncle's title and estates.
His father had left him fifteen thousand pounds, and
his mother about as much more; but this had long ago
gone to the Jews, and Tom was in debt to any amount
you please. His chance of the peerage, however, was
so undeniably safe that he never had the slightest difficulty in borrowing ready money; and it was popularly

believed in Dumplington that Mr. Teasel, the lawyer, whose business was altogether of a mysterious nature, had obligingly accommodated him with several pretty extensive loans. He had first met Edith Montgomery at the county-ball at Dumplington, and before the end of the season they were secretly engaged; secretly, because the old earl had very ambitious views for his heir, and would by no means have consented that he, at any rate, should marry his cook. There was a Lady Maria Bent, daughter of the Duke of Dumplingshire, and sister of the young Marquis of Crookleigh; and Lord Appletree thought what a very nice thing it would be if the two families could be brought together. The duke and the earl divided the county between them; and, as the marquis was a poor, sickly youth, who seemed very unlikely to live, it was highly probable that the fortunate winner of Lady Maria's hand would also be the fortunate possessor of the Dumplingshire ducal estates. But unluckily Lady Maria's hand was not a nice hand to win. It was a large hand, and a red hand, and a very flabby hand. It was the hand of a woman prematurely old, with hair as coarse as ropes, and a parting as broad as a piece of good-sized tape, and an enormous flat face, the color of a swede, and a little round hole for a mouth, and a small, pug nose, and yellow pig's eyes. In short, Lady Maria was a dwarf, and more than half an idiot; and so miserably deformed that not all the lands in Dumplingshire, and the Scotch and Irish properties besides, could put her into shape again. The question with Lord Appletree was, whether she had any need to be put into shape again; whether it would not be worth any man's while who wanted money to take her, hump and all, and make the best of it ; and this question he had proposed for Tom Pippin's consideration, one evening as they rode home together from hunting, a few weeks before he married his cook.

Tom did not like it at all. "By Jove, you know, she is so deucid short, you know, and aw so infernally ugly, you know, and aw really——"

"Well, nobody supposes that she will ever set up for a beauty ; but what of that ? Twelve thousand a year of her own, my boy ; and something like a hundred thousand if young Crookleigh dies."

"Vewy dear at the price," replied Tom, who was thinking of Edith Montgomery. "My dear uncle, I really aw could not think of it."

"I wish you would think of it, Tom, I do indeed. You would feather your nest uncommonly well ; and I don't believe the girl is such a fool as they make her out to be. Besides, a man is not obliged to carry his wife about with him wherever he goes."

But Tom would not hear of it. He had not the least idea that his succession was in danger, and he was a great deal too fond of pretty women to forget Edith, or to enertain without disgust the idea of marrying such a one as Lady Maria. So he turned the tables upon his uncle at last by suggesting that he should bring the two properties together by marrying her himself.

"That's nonsense," said the earl, in a rage ; "utter nonsense, and great impertinence besides. I am not quite such an old fool as that comes to, and I don't think you have any reason for calling me one."

But the earl put the suggestion again to himself as he

was dressing for dinner, and came to the conclusion that though he certainly could not marry Lady Maria Bent, there was no special reason why he should not frighten his nephew into showing a little more respect for his wishes by marrying somebody else. "I am an ugly old beggar, I know," said he, making a face at himself in the glass; "but I have got a good many thousands a year, and if I can find a woman who will be likely to have me, hanged if I won't ask her."

So the earl went down-stairs, and dined tête-à-tête with his nephew Tom. The soup was greasy and cold; the fish was watery; the sweetbread was all gristle and fat, the mutton tough, the pheasant raw, and the bread sauce like a poultice. It was the most villainously bad dinner that ever was put on table, and the earl was very angry indeed. However, he drank his wine like a man; and when Tom Pippin had retired to the smoking-room, after his second or third glass of sherry, he ordered up a pint bottle of claret for his own especial use, and desired that Mrs. Curd, the cook, might be sent up to him.

Mrs. Curd was a long time in obeying the summons, and the earl had finished his claret by the time she knocked at the door. He had not the faintest notion what would come of the interview; no more had she.

He had only seen her once before, when he engaged her: for Lord Appletree attended to all such business himself. "I shall give you thirty pounds a year," he said, "to cook and keep house for me down here. It is but a little place, and I only come for a few weeks in the hunting-season. I shall always expect a nice well-dressed dinner. Good-morning."

On this occasion she had been in her walking costume, and the earl did not take any particular notice of her appearance. But when she came softly into the room, arrayed in evening attire, and dropped a modest curtsy at the door, and then folded her hands with matron-like simplicity upon her little white apron, and waited for further orders, Lord Appletree thought to himself that really, for her station in life, she was not by any means a bad-looking woman.

"Mrs. Curd," he began, "pray what is the reason that I have such abominably bad dinners? I have been nearly poisoned to-night. Everything was as nasty as it could possibly be."

"I am sure, my lord, I am very much surprised to hear it. I never heard any complaints before, and wherever I have lived I have always given satisfaction."

"Then some people are very easily satisfied, that is all I can say. I am not very particular myself, but I cannot eat bread poultices, and if you send me up any more of them, we must part."

"Poultices, my lord! well, I never did! I think I must have misunderstood you, my lord."

"Not in the least, my good woman; only don't let it occur again."

"No, my lord, it shall not occur again; and if your lordship pleases, I should wish to leave. I trust I shall do my duty, go where I will; neether do I desire to be disrespectful neether to master nor mistress; but I could not think of remaining in a house where I have been accused of making poultices, not on the same terms."

"Pooh, nonsense, Mrs. Curd; we shall get on very

well for the future, I dare say. Only I have a particular dislike to poul——I mean, I like my bread sauce
very nicely done."

"I am sure it's very hard," said Mrs. Curd, putting
her hand up to her eyes. "So as I have tried to please,
slaving night and day; and them impudent hussies
of servants down-stairs so troublesome to manage, too.
I thought I had got a nice comfortable place at last.
Oh, deary me!"

"Well, my good creature, don't cry," said the earl,
who could not bear the sight of a woman in tears. "I'll
have another pheasant for dinner to-morrow, and then
we shall be all right, I dare say." And as he spoke
Lord Appletree came close up to the cook, and put his
hand upon her arm.

It was a nice fat soft arm; any one could feel that,
even through the stiff calico sleeve which covered it.
And then it was a very little way from the cook's arm
to the cook's neck, which was fatter and softer still.
So the end of it was that the earl put his arm round the
cook's neck, the wicked old man, and kissed her.

She was a comely-looking woman enough, with nice
red lips and bright blue eyes; and as she did not strug-
gle or make any fuss about being kissed, he kisssd her
again.

"I did not think you would do that, my lord," she
said at last, "and I don't think you had ought to, neether. It is not what I have been used to where I have
lived before, to have such liberties taken, and that I
can tell your lordship."

"No liberty at all, my dear woman," said the earl,
kissing her again, for now that he had begun he did not

like leaving off. "We shall be very good friends now, I am sure; and look here, Susan——"

"My name is not Susan," said Mrs. Curd, drawing herself up with dignity. "It's Martha."

"Well, then, Martha, here is a sovereign for you; and now you can go and get your supper. Good-night." And the old rascal kissed her once more.

Then he sat down and thought about it all, and wondered how he could have been such a fool, at his time of life, as to go kissing a middle-aged woman. And yet Mrs. Curd had been very nice to him. Why should he not kiss her? Why should he not even marry her? There was no reason why he should be a lonely old man for the rest of his life, because he had chosen not to bore himself with a wife until now. Mrs. Curd was not likely to have a family, so it could do no harm to his heir; and if it did, let his heir be hanged. Tom Pippin was nothing to him, that he should succeed him as a matter of course, and play the very devil with the property—for everybody knew what a spendthrift Tom was. People might laugh at him, and abuse him, and even cut him; but what of that? He was great enough and rich enough to be independent of them all; his mind was made up; he would do what many an old man had done before, and marry his cook.

So thought the earl as he sat alone in his easy-chair; and it is to be presumed that Mrs. Curd, as she sat alone in her little housekeeper's room, had her thoughts on the matter too. What did his lordship mean, she should like to know, by kissing of her? A proud old gentleman like him, as didn't seem to think any born lady good enough for him, to go a kissing of his cook!

She should as soon have thought of being kissed by the Prince of Wales. Perhaps he had taken a little too much wine, and yet he seemed sober enough. Well, all she knew was, she would not put up with it, that she wouldn't; and she should give notice in the morning.

The morning came; and, strange to say, the cook and her master were both in the same frame of mind. Resolutions made overnight do not often come to much; but in this case the earl was still determined to marry his cook, and the cook was still determined to protect her dignity by delivering up the housekeeper's keys, and making over the preparation of bread poultices to some more artistic matron.

"Sit down, Martha, if you please," said the earl as she entered the room after breakfast. "I want to have a little conversation with you."

"I should prefer to stand, my lord, if your lordship pleases; and I should desire to be addressed by your lordship as Mrs. Curd."

"Why as *Mrs.* Curd, I should like to know?" said the earl. "You never were married, were you?"

"My lord," answered the cook, beginning to whimper, "I did not come here to be upbraided with the loneliness of my lot, which it have pleased Providence that I should be a spinster, but to give notice to quit your lordship's service this day month. I trust I shall do my duty, go where I will; neether do I wish to be disrespectful neether to master nor mistress; but, after what occurred in this room last night, I could not think of remaining in the house any longer, not upon the same terms."

"Then you shall remain on different terms, my good creature; you shall be my wife. There, you need not jump; I am quite in earnest. Come and give me a kiss."

"No, my lord, you will excuse me, but I know my duty. If your lordship wanted a wife, you would seek one from your own exalted station, and not trifle with the feelings of a homely person like me." And Mrs. Curd, as with befitting dignity she declined her master's offer, nevertheless smiled her prettiest upon him, and contrived, almost imperceptibly, to get herself within reach of his arm; a movement of which Lord Appletree took so base an advantage, that when Tom Pippin entered the room, some fifteen minutes afterwards, he found the cook sitting upon his uncle's knee, with his ugly little pug nose buried in her dainty neck, and his hand pinching her chubby cheeks as if they were all his own.

Of course Tom burst out laughing; there was nothing else for him to do. And of course Mrs. Curd rushed from the room with a scream of mingled terror and triumph, leaving the earl to settle the matter with his heir. As for Lord Appletree, he simply cursed his own stupidity in not having bolted the door, and wished his affectionate nephew any imaginable depth underground.

"What the devil do you mean, sir, by bursting into the room like that?" said the earl, trembling with confusion and rage.

"I am really very sorry," said Tom, laughing still. "I had not an idea you were aw engaged. But, by Jove, that wasn't aw Lady Maria, was it?"

"No, sir, it was not; it was Mrs. Curd, the lady whom I am going to marry," said the earl, thinking the murder might as well come out at once. At any rate, he was not going to be abashed before his own nephew.

"Is she, aw, a Devonshire Curd, one of Lord Junket's people?" asked Tom, languidly throwing himself into a chair.

"No, sir, she is not one of anybody's people. She is at present my cook. This day fortnight she will be my wife."

"By Jove, you must be aw joking, you know. You can't seriously mean to say that you are going to mawwy your cook. It's too ridiculous, you know, ha, ha!" And Tom, regardless of the old man's feelings, roared with laughter.

"It could be nothing to you, sir, if I were going to marry my grandmother."

"Why, that's pwohibited," said Tom. "I remember I used to read about it in church, at the end of the Prayer Book: 'A man may not marry his grandmother.' But you are not in earnest, sir. You would not do a thing to make all the county laugh at you."

"I mean to please myself, sir, let the county laugh as much as it will. And it pleases me to make that woman my wife; unless, Tom, you will oblige me about Lady Maria. I'll give it up, then, I declare I will. I do so want to see the properties brought together."

"Couldn't do it at any price," said Tom; "she is

aw such a frightful creature. I'd aw—yes, by Jove,
I'd sooner marry my coo——''

"Leave the room, you impudent young villain!''
cried the earl; and Tom Pippin, utterly unable, in
spite of his uncle's wrath, to restrain his laughter,
sauntered away.

5

CHAPTER VI.

LORD APPLETREE SEES HIS FRIENDS AT DINNER.

AND so the old Earl of Appletree married his cook,
and had his baby christened, and invited his friends to
make merry with him. Very grand was the dinner-
party on the Monday after the christening. Of course
nobody got anything to eat, it being universally recognized as the sign of a plebeian stomach to feed before
company. Good manners demand that a poor hungry
wretch, who has had no luncheon, and who breakfasted
at eight or nine, shall shake his head impatiently at
half the things the waiter carries round, as if the man
were simply boring him with his odious dishes; and,
when at last he accepts with well-bred indifference a
scrap of mutton about the size of a card-case, shall
"play with his knife and fork," and eat his food in
pretty little morsels as if it were making him sick.
The entire object of dining, in these days of civilization, appears to be to see how soon the good things
can be hurried off the table again. Will anybody
kindly inform me, since persons of refinement clearly
do not eat at dinner-time, when they *do* eat? Do
they gorge at the hour of luncheon? Do ladies forget
themselves over their thin bread-and-butter at five
o'clock, and gentlemen indulge in surreptitious chops

and bitter beer in their dressing-rooms? It may very possibly be vulgar to eat; but life can scarcely be supported without descending to the vulgarity; and I really find it difficult to believe, with reference to the sweet creature whom I have taken in to dinner, who holds the footman and all his dainties in undisguised contempt, and who clearly looks upon me as an ill-conditioned Goth when I modestly ask for another slice off the breast of a chicken—I find it difficult, I confess, to persuade myself that those plump shoulders, and that exquisitely symmetrical bust, are maintained in their fair proportions by lady-like sippings of white soup and trifle.

But, if his guests got nothing to eat, Lord Appletree took care that they should have plenty to drink, and the choicest treasures of his cellar made glad the heart of those assembled to do the young viscount honor. Good wine in moderation, after a good dinner, never yet hurt anybody; but good wine on an almost empty stomach, as one very generally has to drink it, makes some men cross, and some men stupid, and all men more or less disposed to breakfast off soda-water in the morning. Now, Captain Northcote, R.N., of Aleworth, near Dumplington, had drunk a great deal of wine on this particular evening; and the Rev. Robinson Rampion, Rector of Withycombe, Canon of Exeter, Prebendary of Wells, Rural Dean, and Chaplain to Lord Appletree, had drunk a great deal more. They were neither of them anything like tipsy, of course; but they had both arrived at that stage, where language is apt to become personal, and arguments, if they lose in clearness, can hardly be said to lose in point and vigor.

Captain Northcote did not much believe in parsons, and had no particular objection to saying so. He could not quite understand why they should marry wives like other people, eat and drink like other people, and enjoy the good things of this life throughout the week more than most other professional men, and then get up in the pulpit on Sunday and preach for fifty minutes about the blessedness of self-denial, and the heartless vanities of the world. "It's all my eye," said the captain. "If the world is half so wicked as they make it out to be, what business have the parsons to go out to dinner, and crack their jokes over a glass of port wine? I can respect the monk or hermit, who kneels before his crucifix all day long, with clasped hands and streaming eyes. I may think him mistaken, but I can't think him a humbug. Now your modern ascetic parson, with his rich living and his fine-lady wife, *is* a humbug—an unmitigated humbug. He has got all that this world can give him, with the addition of a halo of sanctity borrowed from the world to come; and he growls at you and me because we want to enjoy this world's comforts for the short time they last, and are willing to let him keep the halo of sanctity for himself. In the name of common sense, let us have one thing or the other. If the parsons think so badly of the world, let them renounce it once for all as an unholy thing, separate themselves bodily from women, wine, society, and all that makes this life pleasant, and then preach to us, as men who have earned a right to speak, of another and a better life above. But so long as they do exactly as we sinful laymen do, under pretense of leavening our wickedness with their morality, so long shall we regard them as very good company on Saturday night, and very miserable expounders of a gospel which they have invented for themselves on Sunday."

Captain Northcote was not quite so rude as to say all this to the Rev. Mr. Rampion at Lord Appletree's table; but he said quite enough, in the same strain, to arouse the rector's wrath, and provoke him to declare war.

"Ah," said the captain, speaking of some London clergyman, whose name happened to be just then before the public; "ah—he is something like a parson. I don't believe in his incense and chasubles, because I don't precisely know which is which; but I do believe in his downright hard work, and self-denial, and activity."

"Activity, sir!" broke in the rector. "I *hate* activity. I once had a curate who turned the parish literally upside down with his activity. I had scarcely been away three months——"

"Away three months!" echoed the captain.

"Yes, sir; I hold a canonry at Exeter."

"Oh," said the captain.

"——Before he had gone bustling about among the people, putting all sorts of radical notions into their heads, and making them believe that nobody ever cared about their souls or their bodies either till he came. The consequence was that the moment I returned home a dozen impertinent boys waylaid me at the schoolroom door, and said that they had learned to sing, and bothered me to let them wear surplices in the choir, and chant the Psalms. A very indiscreet

young man was Mr. Burn ;" and here the rector gave
a patronizing glance at his present curate, who sat on
the opposite side of the table, by way of complimenting
him on his discretion.

" It seems to me that you gentlemen are confoundedly hard upon your curates," said the captain. " You
expect them to work, and not to work. It isn't reasonable. If they do a lot of good in the parish, you are
jealous of them ; if they don't do a lot of good, you
sack them. And the way some of them are paid for
their labor—I say, sir, it's diabolical. What do you
think of this, sir ? I know a parson whose living is
worth a thousand a year ; and he gives his curate—
how much do you suppose, now?"

"Really, sir, I have no means of judging ; but
you are not perhaps aware that there are circumstances——"

" I know all about it, sir ; I'll tell you the circumstances. The circumstances are these, sir. The man
has a thousand a year ; and he has the barefaced impudence to give his curate a hundred pounds out of it,
a beggarly tenth part, for doing more than half his
work for him. Do you call that honest, sir? I ask you
plainly, do you call that honest?"

"Come, come, Northcote," interposed Lord Appletree ; for Mr. Toyle, the curate, was in a cold perspira-
tion, and the rector showed manifest symptoms of an
apoplectic fit.

"I say, sir," persisted the captain, rising from his
seat, and getting nearer and nearer to his victim, "I
say that man is a cheat, sir ; a common swindler,
sir !"

"You can scarcely be aware, sir," began the rector, white with rage, "that your remarks——"

"I say, sir, that a man who has solemnly undertaken the most sacred work, and who pays somebody else a beggarly hundred a year to do it for him, ought to be hung—to be hung, sir—I say to be hung!"

"Never you mind him, parson," said Lord Apple-tree. "He does not mean half he says. Come along into the drawing-room, Northcote, that's a good fellow, and drink a cup of tea."

So the guests who were staying in the house went into the drawing-room, while Mr. Rampion was driven home to the rectory, and Mr. Toyle, whose lodgings were in another direction, set off for his solitary walk. Among the many privileges attached to this gentleman's curacy, must certainly be reckoned that of dining out two or three times a week; for Mr. Toyle was hospitably received both at the big house and at the rectory. Everybody was civil and kind to him, asking thoughtfully after his sister, who had once been staying with him on a visit; hoping that the chimney at his lodgings had given over smoking, and that he had not found the bloodhound unchained in the farm-yard since the night when that valuable guardian of property made its teeth meet in the calf of his leg. These were very pleasant evenings to Mr. Toyle. Nobody snubbed him—not even the servants—and nobody bored him to sing; but they all treated him like a gentleman, which he certainly was, and tried to make him feel at home and welcome. There was one little drawback, to be sure,—the walk home at night. For Mr. Toyle, though not a coward, was habitually nervous. I am not sure that from any

bodily peril whatever Mr. Toyle would have run away;
but it did not take much to startle him, and make him
creep, and drive all his breath where it never was meant
to be. Living so much alone had increased, if it did
not originate, this infirmity; and Mr. Toyle had a
strong objection to walking by himself at night along a
lonely lane. It was all very well to go out to dinner;
but there was no particular treat in turning out of a hot
cheerful drawing-room, at eleven o'clock, into a dreary,
and for the most part very dirty, road. "I am afraid
it is a rough night," Lord Appletree would say, when
the curate rose to take leave. "Oh, I do not mind
that, thank you," he would answer; "one soon gets
used to wind and rain." And yet, when John Thomas
had let him out, and he found himself plunging into
the darkness, he felt more inclined to coil himself round
and go to sleep under some laurels in the shrubbery
than to strike across the park, with its gaunt timber
creaking overhead, and to face the horrible lane, with
its murderous-looking copse on the one side, and its
great yawning quarry on the other. But it was not
always dark and rainy. Periodically the curate's walk
home was under a bright sky, and over a hard frosty
road. "You will have a moon to-night," said Mr.
Rampion. "I almost envy you your beautiful walk."
"Do you?" muttered the curate, tying on his scarf;
"then I wish the deuce you'd walk it for me." Beautiful! why, he *hated* the moon, and all the stars together. Groping forward in the dark was bad enough,
but that was nothing to the lights and shadows of a
fine frosty night. Every tree looked as if it had somebody behind it; every gate appeared to be on the

swing; and he knew the road so well that if a sprig of holly were bent out of its place he started and thought there must be something wrong. Besides, there were real and substantial perils in these solitary walks. Had not pedestrians by night, as inoffensive as himself, been garroted, or knocked down with bludgeons? And what should prevent the like from happening to him? All the parish knew where he was gone, and when he would come back again; and, if any needy tramp felt disposed to lay wait for him and tap him on the head, what should hinder him? Such were the curate's agreeable thoughts, as he walked home by moonlight; and will any one declare that such thoughts were unnatural? It is very easy for you, O strong-minded reader, strong in the company of merry laughing children, strong in the cosiness of your bright fireside,—it is very easy for you to smile and sneer, and say that the poor curate was a coward and a fool. But just you wait till the fire is gone out, and the children are safe in bed, and then turn out yourself, and see. There is quite enough of nervousness or superstition about most of us to make a lonely walk at midnight anything rather than agreeable; and the man is simply not to be believed who tells you in a room full of people that he would not mind walking through a churchyard by himself, as the clock strikes the sensational hour of twelve.

> Some folks is brave by candlelight,
> Some folks is brave by day;
> 'Taint many folks is brave by night,
> When the candle's took away.

It's mighty fine to laugh at ghosts ;
  But I always did remark
That them as does screams out with fright
  If you leaves 'em in the dark.

It was a desperately rough night in the early part of
October when the Rev. Ernest Toyle started off for his
homeward walk after Lord Appletree's christening-din-
ner. The elms were bowing themselves backwards and
forwards till the curate thought their trunks must be
made of india-rubber. The wind roared overhead in
a perfect fury, as if the world had been wickeder that
day than usual, and must be well lashed for its naughti-
ness, if not swept clean away. It was as much as the
poor man could do to stand, and a good deal more
than he could do to walk straight before him, even if it
had not been so pitch dark that he could scarcely find
the road. Staggering along sideways like a crab, with
his left hand clutching hold of the brim of his wide-
awake, he ran first into a thorn-bush, secondly into a
heap of something softer but less inviting, and thirdly
into the arms of a great big burly fellow, whom he recognized, before he had time to get frightened, as the
village policeman.

"Good gracious, Cuffs!" he cried, "who ever
thought of meeting you here ! Why, I did not know
that you ever turned out into the country so late as
this."

"No more I doesn't, sir, leastways not commonly ;
but there's such a terrible queer lot of chaps hanging
about just now, along of these here rejoicings, that I've
had a hint from our inspector to keep a eye upon 'em.
So I thought, as this 'ere's a *proper* night for bugglaries,

I'd walk round the great house and see what was going on."

"Dear me!" said the curate, "I hope I sha'n't meet anybody. Why, Cuffs, I've got as much as five-and-twenty sovereigns in my purse at this moment."

"Five-and-twenty sovereigns, Mr. Toyle? that's a large sum of money to carry about with you!"

"It was quarter-day last week, you know, Cuffs," explained the curate, who was by no means certain that the policeman did not suspect him of having picked somebody's pocket in the earl's dining-room. "I changed my check in Dumplington to-day, and brought the sovereigns with me."

"I almost wonder, sir," observed the policeman, "that you did not lock the money up in your desk."

"That was because I had only just time to dress for dinner," said the curate. "Why, my good fellow," he continued, laughing, "you don't really think I stole it, do you?"

"No, sir—no, I don't think that," said the policeman; graciously, indeed, but with an air of judicious reservation befitting a member of her Majesty's Executive. "No, sir, I don't think you stole it."

"Thank you, Cuffs," said the curate. "And now I'll say good-night."

"Would you like me to see you home, sir?" asked the policeman, civilly.

"Oh, lor, no!" said the curate. "I shall do well enough." So he staggered on again, turning out of the road, and following, as best he might, a pathway which led to a corner of the park, where there was a stile, and then a short lane, and then a pond, with a great ash drooping over it, and then a stone-quarry, and then the village green.

He was just getting over the stile, some ten minutes after parting with the policeman, when he saw, leaning against the park palings, the realization of all his horrible dreams and fancies as he had passed that murderous corner. A ruffianly-looking figure with no hat, but a handkerchief bound round its head, and a cudgel in its hand. What a fool he had been to go out to dinner! He would never, never go again! Why had not he crawled into one of Lord Appletree's empty kennels, or borrowed a rug out of the hall and curled himself up in the shrubbery?

He was too much terrified to scream, but he stepped on, his knees almost giving way, and jerked out the most cheerful good-night which under the circumstances he could command. "Good-night," returned the man, as he passed behind him. The curate suspiciously turned round, but only in time to transfer a blow intended for the back of his head to a more dangerous spot behind the ear. It was all over in a moment. Down he went like a rabbit, rolling over to the side of the lane, where he lay, either stunned or dead, till the policeman came back from his rounds, picked him up, and carried him tenderly home.

CHAPTER VII.

CAPTAIN NORTHCOTE PAYS A VISIT.

THE next day there was a sensation in the village of Withycombe. The Rev. Toyle had been thrown into the pond and drowned. The Rev. Toyle had had his throat cut in Hangman's Lane. The Rev. Toyle had had his brains blown out by Lord Appletree's under-keeper. The Rev. Toyle had been killed on the spot by the fall of a tree in the park, coming home from dinner. It was a shame, it was, to leave them rotten elms a standing. His lordship ought to be persecuted for it, so he did. If he was a poor man, he would not be allowed to go putting people's lives in danger, no more he wouldn't. Opinions therefore differed as to the exact manner in which the Rev. Toyle had come to his untimely end; though nobody ventured to dispute the fact that, somehow or other, the untimely end had been successfully attained.

But the Rev. Toyle disappointed them all, and took the tragedy of his own decease clean out of their mouths, by keeping his shutters open and his blinds drawn up, and turning out to be alive. It was very inconsiderate. It was scarcely like a gentleman. Had the poor curate died, the whole village would have wept, and wept sincerely too; but, now that he was

come to life again, it did seem rather hard that everything should be humdrum, and the little world of
Withycombe should go plodding on precisely as before. We all have our facetious little ways. We entertain the highest possible regard for our dear friend Robinson, and certainly wish our neighbor Jones no harm;
and yet it was rather good fun to hear one morning,
when news was somewhat slack, that Brown had run
away with Robinson's pretty wife, and that Jones could
not pay his debts, and was obliged to leave the town.
Even the weeping child who has lost her mother derives
consolation in her grief from the dear little black frock
which the dressmaker has just brought home. If her
mother could come back again, no doubt she would be
very glad to see her; but, as her mother can't, it will
really be very nice to go to church on Sunday, and
show off all the new crape trimmings.

So the curate turned out to be alive, and was reported
as such by Mr. Cuffs the policeman, when he laid information of the outrage before Lord Appletree at
breakfast-time on Tuesday morning.

"And have you no clue whatever, Cuffs?" asked his
lordship, as he helped himself to a deviled kidney,
from a little round silver dish on three spider's legs.

"None whatever, my lord," replied the policeman,
"except this 'ere empty purse, which I found lying on
some weeds beside the pond. I conclude it do belong to Mr. Toyle, as he told me that he had some
money about him;" and then the servant of the
Crown narrated his meeting with the curate the night
before.

"So he told you that he had five-and-twenty pounds

about him, did he?" observed Captain Northcote, indifferently.

"Yes, my lord, he did," replied the policeman,
under the natural impression that the breakfast-party
was made up of aristocrats all round. It is nice to say
"my lord." One shines with borrowed luster in the
presence of noble earls; and better men than Mr.
Cuffs have conferred imaginary titles upon themselves,
by plentifully my-lording the mighty potentate with
whom they have been permitted to converse.

"Ah," said the captain, indifferently still; and then
Mr. Cuffs was formally instructed to get some breakfast
down-stairs, and to lose no time in tracking out, with
all professional craft and diligence, the perpetrator of
last night's assault.

After breakfast the young people rehearsed their
theatricals for the evening; and Tom Pippin, who was
an accomplished manager as well as a first-rate actor,
busied himself in superintending the erection of a stage.
Meanwhile, Captain Northcote walked down into the
village, and asked his way to the curate's rooms. They
were kept by a certain widow Giles, a woman with a
most awful tongue, who led her lodger such a life as
only British curates can endure. She fed him well,
and gave him plenty of light and air; and, if she
would only have let the wretched man alone, he might
have had some chance of comfort. But no. She
dodged him in the passage, knocked incessantly at his
door, waylaid him in his going out and coming in,
hovered over him with questions which interested
neither him nor her, and altogether pitilessly bored
him. She would chase him all round the garden to

tell him that the coals could not last more than a fortnight longer; and hunt him down, when he had fled
in desperation to his bedroom, to say that the baker
had charged him a halfpenny too much in his weekly
bill. It is thus that well-intentioned matrons make
bachelors' lives a burden, and force them, in sheer self-
defense, to embark upon a sea of unknown perils.

"A bad business, ma'am," observed the captain, as
the widow let him in.

"Ah sir that it is indeed. I never was so shocked
in all my born days as I was a saying just now to Mr.
Toyle."

"I should have supposed, ma'am, that the less said
to Mr. Toyle just now the better," said the captain,
civilly.

"Oh lor bless you sir he like to hear anybody talk
he do I've been a cheering of him up for ever so long
a telling of him how my poor boy that died of brain
fever got a crack on his head at——"

"Yes, I dare say it was a great comfort to him,
ma'am; but could I see him for a minute or two? I
am sure he must want rest, so I won't keep him long."

"I'll see sir I make no doubt but you can," answered
the good lady, going up-stairs and knocking at the
bedroom door. Having admitted herself, she bustled
about for a few minutes "to tidy up a bit," and then
returned to let the captain in.

"I should like to see the gentleman *alone*," said the
captain, perceiving that widow Giles had no present
idea of leaving the room. Then, walking quietly up
to the bedside, he shook the sick man's hand, and
made the customary inquiries.

"A little shaky about the head, thank you," replied the curate. "If I could only keep that woman out of the room, I should soon come round again."

"By Jove, sir, you have had a near shave of it!" said his visitor, looking at the wound. "It's an uncommonly nasty place, by George, it is; and you may thank God it's no worse," added the gallant captain, whose mythology took a somewhat extensive range.

"I was a great fool to let him hit me," said the curate. "I ought to have turned round sharper, and let out at him."

"So you ought, sir, and so you will, another time, I'll be bound. You haven't any suspicion who it was, I suppose?"

"Not the slightest in the world. The fellow was muffled up to the very eyes."

"Ah, it is just as well not to suspect anybody. You never hope to see your money again, of course?"

"Indeed, I do," said the curate. "We have a policeman living in the village, you know; an awfully sharp fellow. I shall be very much surprised, and, I am bound to say, terribly disappointed, if he does not get it back for me."

"*Very* sharp, I should say he was," returned the captain. "I saw him this morning, and he has gone off in chase. But if he brings the thief home to-night, or to-morrow night, or any other night, I'll swallow him."

"Dear me," said the curate, "what makes you think so?"

"Think so! I don't think anything about it. You'll never get a farthing of that money back again, and, what is more, the robber will never be brought to

6

justice. It was about the cleverest dodge I ever heard of. But I did not come here, sir, to console you by telling you that. I came to ask a favor of you. Five-and-twenty sovereigns is a good lot of money, but it is not quite so much to me, perhaps, as it is to you; so, as I am prepared to take my oath that you will never get your own again, will you let me make it up to you? Here it is, you see," continued the captain, pushing some notes under the pillow, as the curate turned his head away. "I'll look in again to-morrow, if I may, and bring Lord Appletree down. We will tell you how the theatricals went off. Horrid bore that you can't get up and see them. Good-by." And, before the sick man could recover his voice and thank him, the captain had left the room.

The promised visit was paid on the Wednesday morning, when Lord Appletree accompanied the captain, and took the chief blame of Mr. Toyle's misfortune upon himself.

"It was my fault," declared the earl, "for sending you home so late. I'll never do such an inhospitable thing again. You shall have a snug little room kept on purpose for you, Toyle, and I hope you will come and sleep in it three times every week, at least, while we are here. But if ever you *should* have to walk at midnight in the country again, let me advise you, as a friend, to leave your purse behind you, and take a good big stick instead."

"And let *me*," added the captain, "advise you, as a friend, if ever you *should* have to walk at midnight in the country again, with five-and-twenty sovereigns in your pocket,—let *me* advise you—not to tell the policeman."

CHAPTER VIII.

MR. GOGGS GIVES BREAD TO THE HUNGRY.

Long before the celebration of the festivities at
Withycombe House, the Rev. Mr. Goggs had obtained
his appointment from the trustees of Woodruff's Charity, and had set up in business as a boy-farmer on a
tolerably extensive scale.

The "charity" consisted in boarding and educating
twelve boys, natives of the county, for nothing : the
master being supposed to provide for their necessities
out of his official salary of five hundred pounds a year.
These boys were distinguished from their more profitable school-fellows visibly by a square cap with a white
tassel, and invisibly by the peculiar consideration and
kindness which they received at the hands of Mr. and
Mrs. Goggs.

When old Simon Woodruff, about the year 1402,
devised certain dwelling-houses, in or near the good
city of Dumplington, with lands adjoining thereunto,
for the free maintenance of twelve poor scholars forever, he could have had but little idea with what scru-
pulous fidelity his injunctions would be obeyed. The
" founder's boys" at Dumplington were maintained not
only free of cost, but free even of decent food—free
of bedclothes enough to keep their bodies warm—free

of every common civility to which ordinary mortals
are permitted to lay claim.   Generation after generation of schoolmasters had bullied them, and spited
them, and visited upon them, innocent or guilty, every
conceivable crime committed in the school.   Generation after generation of schoolmistresses had starved
them, and physicked them, and snubbed them, and
snarled at them, and sneaked of them to the master
for every little trumpery fault, and made them to know
how blessed a thing it is to be the recipient of a charity, and how high the privilege of being boarded and
educated " free."

Periodically, when some speculator of a more adventurous turn than usual had charge of the farm, the delicate attentions paid to the founder's boys were apt to
be overdone, and a case which would have been given
as manslaughter against any one else but a schoolmaster
attracted public notice for awhile.   But now, at the
period of Mr. Goggs's appointment, all that sort of
thing was happily exploded.   No clergyman could
venture in these days to ill treat a pupil; and if any
founder's boy at Dumplington had dared to tell his
friends that he was not fed like a prince and petted
like a poodle, the ungrateful little wretch would have
had his ears well boxed, and have been sent back to
school at the end of the holidays with a basket of
game for his kind master and a sucking-pig for his
kind mistress, and a letter expressing the deep sense
which his parents entertained of the affectionate soli-
citude of Mr. and Mrs. Goggs.

Among those who had committed their sons to Mr.
Goggs's care were Mr. Nightshade, the undertaker,

Mr. Teasel, the lawyer, and Captain Northcote, R.N.,
of Aleworth, near Dumplington. Mr. Nightshade, as
a tradesman in the town, had a right to a free nomina-
tion for his boy. Mr. Teasel, in virtue of his long
residence, enjoyed an equal right, if he had chosen to
press it ; but the founder's boys, with casual exceptions
here and there, had from time immemorial been held
in such contempt by the rest of the school that it answered the lawyer's purpose better to send his son as a
day-scholar, paying for his education, in return for
having jobbed the head-master into office, less than
half the customary charge. Captain Northcote was not
specially fond of Mr. Goggs, though he failed perhaps
to see through his pious relation with his wonted acute-
ness ; but there were two good and sufficient reasons
why he should select Dumplington Grammar-School
for his son. In the first place, his wife had labored
under the delusion, by which many fond mothers are
afflicted, that public schools are hells upon earth, where
one half of the smaller boys catch malignant fever, and
the other half are roasted alive. She had implored,
therefore, just before she died, that the precious child
she was leaving behind her might never be subjected
to such perils ; and her husband was not the sort of
man to forget, any number of years afterwards, that
such a request had been made. Much as he wished it,
he could not bring himself to send Harry to a public
school ; and, if he *must* descend to an academy, it
seemed only gracious to do a neighborly turn for Mr.
Goggs, who, but for an unlucky chance, might now be
in possession of half the fortune left to his boy by the
old brewer. Thus it came to pass that Harry North-

cote went to Dumplington to be farmed; where his
father, by stipulating that he should have cold meat or
an egg for breakfast, made an excuse to pay for his
schooling a hundred and fifty guineas a year.

These three boys were continual objects of petty
spitefulness to Mr. and Mrs. Goggs: Harry Northcote, because he had choused them out of a legacy;
Frank Teasel, because his father only paid five pounds
a year; and Willie Nightshade, because he was on the
foundation, and his father paid nothing at all. It is
only fair to say that each of the three manifested a
touching appreciation of favors conferred, and led
their indulgent master and mistress such a life that Mr.
Goggs was under the habitual necessity of strengthen-
ing himself with bottled porter before going into school,
while the nerves of his invalid wife were so perpetually
unstrung as to render beef-tea and calves'-foot jelly
essential at all hours of the day, and force her poor
weak system to undergo the stimulating influence of
port wine, before she could summon up energy enough
to ladle out the hash at dinner.

Port wine was not the only luxury with which Mr.
and Mrs. Goggs had the good taste to set the boys'
mouths watering at meal-time. When they first began
farming, and still retained some of the foolish sensitive-
ness of ordinary beings, they had been accustomed to
eat a bit of bread and cheese in the dining-hall at one
o'clock, and dine by themselves in the evening. The
servants, however, grumbled at the late dinner; and an
invaluable cook, who was wont to salt the boiled beef
so effectually that the boys could not possibly eat more
than one helping of it, and had a knack of swelling

out the grains of rice till they were almost as big as beans, gave warning to leave that day month. But, before even that day fortnight arrived, Mr. and Mrs. Goggs had foregone their evening banquet, and were dining at one o'clock in the hall.

"It will be very awkward, my dear," said Mrs. Goggs. "We have a roast duck for dinner to-day, and the boys will be sure to smell it."

"Let 'em smell it!" returned Mr. Goggs, angry at the loss of his quiet meal, and rapidly becoming hardened in the little refinements of his calling. "Let 'em smell it. It's very wholesome for them. There's nothing so good for little boys as to smell something nice, and have to eat something nas——I mean, ar—— something nutritious and—ar——satisfying. Depend upon it, my dear, a child cannot begin too soon to conquer his appetite, and put a restraint upon his vile affections. But the second bell is ringing. Let us go into the hall, and ask a blessing upon our simple meal."

The simple meal consisted of a cut of salmon, with cucumber and lobster sauce; followed by a roast duck, with green peas and salad, and bitter beer. The boys, who had been playing cricket under a broiling sun for three-quarters of an hour, were refreshed by some highly desirable soup, manufactured by the invaluable cook out of hot water, dripping, pearl barley, salt, and pepper. After this, they fed sumptuously on veal pie, the crust of which no mortal teeth could penetrate, while the meat was contributed by a calf of so remarkable a texture that you felt as if the creature must have died hard, and wondered whether the entire animal, hide, hoofs, and incipient horns, had been made to minister to your bodily sustenance. There was no pudding, it being a "soup" day; but, in place thereof, the boys were permitted to sit in silence for a quarter of an hour, contemplating the Rev. Mr. Goggs as he devoured, with much noise and unclean feeding, a hundred or so of asparagus, cut from the garden for his especial gratification. When this was finished, he and his wife consumed between them a sweet omelet, making over to the two ushers a suet-pudding, flavored with an infinitesimal quantity of gooseberry jam; after which a double Gloucester cheese was set upon the table, and the boys, at a given signal, rose and returned thanks for what they had received, and what they had smelt, and what they had hungrily wished for, and what they certainly would never get, so long as Mr. Goggs continued to be their farmer, and his amiable lady vouchsafed to exercise over them her more than maternal care.

This maternal care was never more judiciously displayed than when any of the younger boys received a "grub parcel" from home. Those only who have themselves been boys at a good, big school can possibly imagine the intense delight with which the hamper is discovered in the passage after breakfast, and is carried off to some quiet spot, and opened with the proprietor's own hands, while its contents are impatiently stripped of the paper in which the neat housekeeper has enveloped them, and are transferred to the playbox, to be distributed at convenient seasons among a select company of friends. But Mrs. Goggs did not appreciate any such delights as these. So, when a parcel arrived at Dumplington, packed carefully by

some little fellow's mother, in anticipation of the glee
with which he would cut the string with his broken
knife, and dive into the depths of his treasure to search
out the tongue, and make sure whether there really was
a cold plum-pudding after all, the considerate schoolmistress would save him the trouble by opening the
hamper herself, and telling the child a day or two afterwards, when the cake was stale, that he might have
half of it at the end of the week, if he were a good
boy.

"Northcote," she said one morning after prayers,
"a parcel came for you yesterday. I suppose you have
been writing home and telling your father that you
don't get enough to eat and drink at school, haven't
you?"

Harry could not say that he hadn't, and he did not
dare to say that he had; so he said nothing, and left
Mrs. Goggs to infer just whatever she pleased.

"Ah, I thought so," she whined out, as if she were
a victim of the grossest ingratitude, and altogether
cruelly misunderstood. "I am sure you have the best
of everything, and I don't approve of your being made
bilious by all these luxuries from home. There are
some apples at the top of the hamper which you can
have this evening if you like; and if you will come
and ask me to-morrow, just before dinner, I will give
you part of the cake." But Harry Northcote, though
he liked cake as much as any other boy, and was dying
of curiosity to see his hamper, would rather go without
food for the rest of his life than ask Mrs. Goggs for it.
There was not one single fellow in the school who would
approach within sight of the woman, if he could possibly

keep away. The boys would endure any amount of pain rather than go up to her and say that they were ill ; not for fear of medicine, but for fear of her disagreeable grating voice and horrid scowl. Delicate little fellows would shiver in their drenched socks till bedtime, rather than ask her to let them go up-stairs and change ; not because they dreaded the inevitable five hundred lines apiece, when she had reported them to the master for getting wet, but because they would not face her repulsive visage, and subject themselves to one of her odious "jaws." Harry Northcote, therefore, left her to do with his hamper precisely as she chose ; but he begged his father, when he went home for the holidays, to bring his next "grub parcel" into Dumplington himself, and deliver it with his own hands, instead of sending it by the carrier.

These little contrivances for keeping their pupils in good health and in a wholesome state of discipline were not, however, always so successful. It happened on a certain half-holiday, about a year after Harry had gone to school, that Frank Teasel, when he went home to dinner, got leave to take two of his friends with him, to spend the afternoon. When the boys had finished supper, and were getting up to say good-by, Mrs. Teasel, who would have stripped the gown off her back to give a hungry child a dinner, insisted on their carrying off with them such portable dainties from the table as their pockets would hold. Harry stowed away half a dozen oranges, and about a pound of brawn ; while the other boy contented himself with a good-sized piece of cheese, a French roll, and a few slices of ham—both of them reluctantly admitting, after much earnest consideration of the matter, that the apple-pie and stewed pears could not be conveniently disposed of, and must be left behind. When they reached the school, Mr. Goggs met them in the passage, asked them what they were carrying, declared that he would not allow such messes to be brought into his house, took all the spoil away, and bestowed it in the morning upon the shoe-black—a wretched youth who, for about eighteen pence a week, brushed—not to say cleaned—the boots of the entire establishment, besides filling coal-scuttles, drawing water, and doing an infinity of odd jobs in the garden. When school was over, Frank went to his father's office, and told him all about it; and in the course of half an hour Mr. Teasel and Mr. Goggs were exchanging compliments in the latter gentleman's study, in a tone of voice so loud that the boys could hear almost every word that passed between them.

" It's as clear a case of stealing, sir," said the lawyer, "as ever I heard of; and I'll trouble you to make restitution. If you don't, you shall be proceeded against just as any other thief, by George you shall!"

" Stealing !" echoed the schoolmaster, lifting up his hands, but not to bless his visitor. " Stealing ! You forget yourself, sir. I am a minister of religion. It is my place to preach to *you*, that *you* should not steal. For, what saith the Scripture? Woe unto you, lawyers——"

" Now look here, Mr. Goggs. We won't have any of that, if you please. It's bad enough to be forced to sit it out on a Sunday; but I'll be shot if I stand it on a weekday. Lawyers, indeed! why, if I had not a clearer conscience than you have, with fifty half-starved

children on your hands. I'd turn watchman, for it
wouldn't be a bit of good to go to bed at night. The
case is simple enough. I have given to two young gentlemen, my guests, certain articles of food from my
table. You, with consummate impudence, have taken
the said articles away, and have given them to somebody else. Now, I don't grudge the wretched shoeblack his breakfast. You may take your oath it's the
first time he has tasted anything nice since he has
been in *your* employment; unless, indeed, you have
been carrying on these little clerical pilferings before.
Besides, I'll be bound to say that Mrs. Goggs will de-
duct the value of the food from the poor beggar's
wages. But I don't choose to be made a fool of; and,
what is more, I don't choose to see two schoolboys
deliberately robbed. I haven't much idea what the
things may have been worth—I suppose about a couple
of shillings. You give the two boys a shilling apiece,
and apologize to me or to my wife for appropriating our
gifts, and we will say no more about it. Otherwise,
I'll be hanged if I don't bring an action."

"Your language, sir," observed Mr. Goggs, who was
white with rage, "is that of an unhappy man, who has
not yet learned to bring his temper into subjection.
The unregenerate nature——"

"All right, old chap. You can put that into your
next discourse, and make your 'message of love' extra
charitable thereby. Only don't let us have it here.
The question is, not whether you are more regenerate
than I am, or whether, which is probable enough, we
are both going to the bad together; not whether farming a set of hungry helpless boys is a lawful and godly

trade, and making a fair profit out of silly clients, who at any rate are old enough to protect themselves, is fiendish and detestable. But the question is, are you going to pay these youths the value of their oranges and rolls, and apologize to me or my wife for stealing them?"

"Certainly not, sir," answered the schoolmaster, with an assumption of dignity which did not impress his visitor with any considerable awe. "Certainly and most emphatically not. Think, sir, how I should forfeit my authority! Consider the discipline which, in humble dependence upon divine grace, it is my duty to maintain! No, sir, I cannot apologize."

"Then you shall be prosecuted as a thief," said the lawyer, putting on his hat, and opening the door. "And if your authority has to be upheld by prigging cold meat and bread and cheese out of your pupils' pockets, I don't think much of it. The day after to-morrow, sir, I go to town on business, and my wife goes with me; but we shall both be at home again this day week: so I give you until that time to think the matter over. Good-morning, Mr. Goggs. Pray don't come out. A thief, mind. It's a criminal case, not a civil action. As a thief, Mr. Goggs—a common thief."

CHAPTER IX.

MR. GOGGS KEEPS COMPANY WITH HIS PIG.

HARRY NORTHCOTE had rather a rough time of it in school that afternoon, for his conscientious master took unusual pains to improve his mind. Mr. Goggs's notion of teaching was, to say the least, peculiar. The boys lolled on a form in front of him, with their heads between their knees, and their legs spread out in readiness to telegraph gentle kicks to one another, or to trip up on his journey any young gentleman who might be so far favored as to be sent to the top of the class, or so far spited as to be sent to the bottom. While Mr. Goggs was looking out words in the dictionary, which his imperfect memory, or defective education in the learned tongues, obliged him to do continually, there was a general bear-fight until the correct "rendering" had been ascertained. If his attention were fixed for a time on one end of the row, the lads at the other end exchanged salutations, after the manner of schoolboys, by pulling their neighbor's hair, upsetting one another off the form, and manifesting other signs of playfulness; until the master, poor fool, suddenly woke up from his state of abstraction, and turned round with an intimation that there was "rather too much noise." Rather too much noise! Probably there

might be. It was one incessant hubbub all day long.
Mr. Goggs had about as good an idea of keeping boys
in order as he had of keeping the stars in their courses.
And here it may be parenthetically observed that the
schoolmaster who is a bully, and a farmer, and a screw,
is perfectly certain to be a bad teacher as well. You
might naturally suppose it to be otherwise. You might
think that one who is severe in exacting impositions
would be severe and strict all round ; that he who is a
brute in his punishments would frighten the boys into
doing their best in school ; and that a man who has
made his pupils hate the very sound of his voice would
at any rate have the faculty of maintaining discipline.
But it is not so. The sympathizing, kindly, genial
master, who would give his eyes to be a boy again ;
who delights in his work, for the interest it brings him,
and towards whom, in his boyish troubles, every little
fellow turns as towards a home friend : this is the man
who keeps order in school, and gets his lessons learned,
and makes his pupils scholars. Boys do not dare to
trifle with such a man, because they can see that he
means business, and will be minded ; and they would
not trifle with him if they dared, because he has won
their hearts by showing that he understands them, and
by treating them as Christian boys, as reasonable beings,
and as gentlemen. But the modern clerical representa-
tive of Mr. Wackford Squeers—the man who keeps a
school just as he might keep a shop, and would embark
in some other business to-morrow if he thought he could
make a pound or two more ; the farmer, who has a flock
of boys to get his living by, but, so long as they pay
him well, does not care whether they feed or starve ;

such a one as this may scatter his pupils into corners
at the sound of his footstep, or drive the blood from
their cheeks by the rapping of his cane, but he will
never terrify them into showing him the commonest
respect, and, what is more, he will never get them to
do half an hour's honest work for him in school.

Mr. Goggs's mood varied according to the time of
day. Before breakfast he was cold and cross, and
much disposed to quicken circulation both in himself
and others by a plentiful use of the stick. After breakfast he was uniformly dyspeptic, the kidneys and
sausages and pigs' feet which the boys had seen him
eat, as they wrestled with their lumps of bread and tal-
low, not agreeing with him so early in the morning.
Towards the middle of the day, however, he brightened
up, and essayed to remember a good many very stale
and very mild jokes, at which he himself laughed pro-
digiously, becoming very angry if the whole form did
not laugh as well. After dinner he went to sleep and
dropped his book, at which signal the boys played the
fool till he woke up again; which he generally did just
as two young gentlemen were in the act of changing
jackets, or indulging in a quiet game of beggar-my-
neighbor behind another young gentleman's back.
Then he rose like a giant refreshed, and laid about
him manfully, almost always thrashing the wrong boys;
after which he stood up to a great blackboard with a
piece of chalk in his hand, and became so hopelessly
involved in blundering through a proposition in Euclid
that the boys gave him up in despair, and simply
yawned in his face, taking their chance of his fury.
This was the man in whom the trustees of Woodruff's

Charity had secured a veritable treasure; of whom examiners, twice every year, made flattering reports; to whom parents wrote gushing letters, brimful of confidence in his management of their darlings. "A most excellent schoolmaster," said all the good folks at Dumplington; "admirably fitted for his post. And as for Mrs. Goggs, there never was a woman like her. She absolutely *devotes herself* to the boys." Poor little beggars! she did, indeed. Devoted herself to interfering with every pleasure they could possibly enjoy; devoted herself to the weighing out of every ounce they swallowed, and every coal that was burned to keep the fire alight in their schoolroom stove. If she had cut their scraps of beef a little bigger, and "devoted herself" a little less, it might have been better for them—and for her. And if the "excellent schoolmaster" had insisted on having his work done properly when it was time to work, and set fewer impositions when it was time to play, his boys would have looked healthier and happier, and he himself would have earned his money from their parents more like an honest man.

"Northcote!" shouted Mr. Goggs, before breakfast on the morning after Mr. Teasel's threat of legal proceedings,—"Northcote! what are you doing?"

"Nothing, sir," said Harry, looking innocently up from his book, on the fly-leaf of which he was sketching Mrs. Goggs, as she appeared in her garden bonnet, stooping down to sort out rotten apples for the boys' dinner.

"Then write out five hundred lines, for doing nothing. You ought to be learning your Ovid."

"Please, sir, I've got fifteen hundred to do already."

"Then you must stop in till they are finished," said Mr. Goggs. "If they are not all shown up by Monday morning at nine o'clock, you will be caned."

"Oh, please, sir," expostulated Harry, giving the final touch to Mrs. Goggs's legs, which he had fashioned after a decidedly bucolic type, and displayed in all their native elegance so far as was consistent with propriety.

"Bring me that book directly," said Mr. Goggs, opening his desk, and fumbling about for a good strong cane.

Harry took this opportunity to open *his* desk, and bring out another book, which he presented to his intelligent relative, who was none the wiser. This volume was also embellished with illustrations, but they were chiefly profiles of schoolfellows, or scenes from the tranquil life of the Dumplington French Master. Mr. Goggs tore out the leaves, and crumpled them up, after which he flew at Harry, and crumpled *him* up, forcing the poor boy's body into such a position that all the blows fell foul, some on his thigh, some on his shoulders, and some on his head.

"I'll teach you, sir!" said Mr. Goggs, hissing out the well-known formula, as the boy, too proud to cry, but too sorely wounded to walk straight, staggered back to his seat. And all this, because Mrs. Teasel had given him some oranges and brawn.

After breakfast the schoolmaster went at him again.

"Northcote," said he, "Mrs. Goggs reports you for leaving a quantity of crumbs in your bed this morning. What have you been eating up-stairs?"

"Only a few biscuits, sir, that I had in my pocket."

"You know very well that it is against the rules," said Mr. Goggs, "to eat anything in your bedroom. You get plenty of good food at meal-times, and if you want more, you have only to ask for it. Why didn't you tell Mrs. Goggs that you were hungry?"

Harry scarcely knew which idea was the most ridiculous—that of getting good food in hall, of asking for anything extra, or of volunteering for any purpose whatever to approach Mrs. Goggs. So he laughed at all three ideas, and more than half the school laughed with him.

"Come here, sir!" cried the master, in a rage. "How dare you giggle in my face? Hold out your hand!"

What with fives, and cricket, and rounders, and various other uses to which they were applied, Harry Northcote's hands were tolerably well seasoned; and yet Mr. Goggs contrived to cut them both open, and set them bleeding, and maim the boy's fingers to an extent which effectually prevented the writing of impositions, at any rate for that day. Bless your soft heart, dear reader, there is no cruelty practiced in modern schools! Nobody nowadays is fool enough to believe that a master ever ill treats a boy! Your boy will say that he has been unjustly punished, of course; but he is an interested witness, and boys tell such shocking lies. Ask the schoolmaster. He is a clergyman, you know, and you will get the truth from *him*. *He* can have no possible interest in making himself out to be the kindest and most patient of men.

Ask him whether his very soul does not overflow with tenderness and loving care. He will set your mind at rest in a moment. The boy's wicked misrepresentations will recoil upon his own head, and he will be thoroughly well thrashed again, as a warning to his schoolfellows, for telling tales.

Harry could not hold his knife and fork at dinner, so Mrs. Goggs cut up his greasy mutton for him. What a kind motherly woman she was! Who else would have taken such trouble for a good-for-nothing lad who was always whistling along the passage, and banging doors, and shattering her delicate nerves?

In the afternoon Harry had a visitor—a most welcome visitor. Tom Pippin, who lived a few miles off, had driven into Dumplington on business; and at five o'clock Harry found him waiting outside the school-room door. Tom Pippin was mincing and affected with men and women, but he was always genuine with boys. The Dumplington fellows delighted in him; not because he tipped them, and brought them good things to eat, or even because he was such a "tremendous swell" at cricket, could run a mile in four minutes and fifty seconds, and jump a foot higher than any chap in the school. But they liked him because he was a "regular downright jolly brick;" and if the reader does not know what that means, he had better go to school again, for there is no other place where he can possibly learn. Tom remembered his boy-English—that lovely dialect which most of us forget as soon as our beards begin to grow. Tom understood boys and their ways; made himself a boy among them; imagined it just conceivable that they might have a grain or two of sense ; and did not sneer at them and snub them because they were a few years younger than himself. And so they loved him ; but Harry North- cote loved him best of all. Tom was his very especial friend—his model—his hero. In Harry's eyes, Tom could do everything better than any one else that ever was born. In Tom's eyes, Harry was the noblest boy that ever breathed ; and if he had chanced to come to the schoolroom door at ten o'clock instead of at five, and had seen Mr. Goggs thrashing his young friend, Mr. Goggs's farming days would probably have been brought to a somewhat abrupt conclusion.

Tom was not alone, for he took about with him, wherever he went, an enormous dog, which he had long ago given to Harry, but which he was keeping for the boy until he had left school. Nobody knew much about the creature's breed ; but Tom had brought him from Russia, and he was supposed to have passed his dog-infancy in chasing wolves. Now that he was full grown, he was fit to chase a tiger ; and the very wag- ging of his tail displayed a muscularity which kept you at a respectful distance behind him. Many and many a happy day had his young master spent in romping with him, when staying at Tom's little country-house in the holidays. For Harry always passed a week at Chrismas and midsummer with his friend, and enjoyed his visit as only a boy of fourteen knows how. It is the fashion with some people to pretend that anybody, if he pleases, can be thoroughly happy anywhere ; that money, and kind friends, and dogs, and ponies, have nothing to do with real enjoyment, but that the eldest of eleven chil- dren, with a slice of bread and dripping for his tea, and only his father's worn-out clothes to wear, is capable of supporting existence quite as cheerfully as the juvenile possessor of all juvenile good things. You often hear such theories put forth with great unction from the pulpit, though you know for certain all the time you listen that the preacher does not believe a word he is saying, and that the congregation don't believe a word they hear. Whether it be wise and right to indulge overmuch in the pleasure that money brings, is another question altogether; but to say that money does not bring pleasure, and downright real delightful pleasure, too, is to say what is not only untrue, but most mischievous besides. Nothing can be more likely to make a boy grow up selfish and luxurious than to tell him that every little country lad who opens the gate for him as he rides past is as well off and as happy as himself; whereas if you teach him something, and perhaps show him something, of the hard hungry life of the poor, there is a chance that he will give them kind words and sixpences when he is a boy, and not forget their struggling poverty when he becomes a man.

"Why, Harry, old boy!" said Tom, as his friend jumped into his arms, "what's the matter with your hands?" And then Frank Teasel and Willie Nightshade, talking both together, told him all about it; Harry finding that his voice failed him, and that, though he could take his thrashing manfully at the time, he could not recount his sufferings without feeling very much disposed to blub. A boy of fourteen will laugh at pain; but he will cry like a little child if you touch his heart by showing him kindness.

" The brute !" exclaimed Tom. " What will you give me, Harry, to polish him off?"

"There he is," said Frank Teasel, as the reverend schoolmaster looked in at the door.

" What a dirty-looking beggar !" observed Tom, who, though he had often paid a visit to the school, had never seen the master before. " Does he ever wash himself, do you think ?"

" Wash !" exclaimed half a dozen fellows at once, "not he ! You should see his nails. And I know for a fact that he makes one flannel shirt and two collars last him for a fortnight."

" What's his name ?" asked Tom.

" Goggs," replied the boys.

" Oh, yes, I remember ; but you don't call him that, I suppose. What's his nickname ?"

" Nickname ! we had no need to give him one. Why, *Goggs* is nickname enough for anybody, isn't it ?"

" Ha, ha !" laughed Tom, delighted. " But I say, Harry, and you, too, Willie and Frank, I want you to come to dinner to-night at the Red Lion. By Jove, I should like to have the whole lot of you ; but old Goggs wouldn't give leave. Cut and ask him, Harry."

Harry shook his head. " Might as well ask him to jump a hurdle," he said at last—hitting upon the most absurdly improbable use to which Mr. Goggs's athletic frame could be applied.

" Tell him you want to go to a missionary meeting," suggested Tom, who had been made aware of Mr. Goggs's piety.

" He is going to one himself to-night," said Frank.

"I saw the bills stuck up in the town. Rev. Goggs in the chair."

"The deuce he is!" said Tom. "Let us all be taken serious and go. What a lark it would be to get near the door, and let in a lot of roughs!"

"If you kick up such a thundering row," said Willie Nightshade, "he'll be in again, as sure as fate."

"Let him," said Tom. "If he so much as pokes his nose in at the door, I swear I'll set Grab at him." And the words were scarcely off his lips, when Mr. Goggs appeared.

"There is too much noise in here," observed that gentleman. "Mrs. Goggs is out of health, and has gone to lie down. I shall give a thousand lines to any boy who makes any further disturbance."

"Fetch him out, Grab!" whispered Tom Pippin, hiding himself behind the stove, and putting his mouth close to the dog's ear. "Fetch him out, old fellow!"

Away bounded Grab, rushing along the whole row of desks, upsetting slates, exercise-books, and dictionaries; and away went Mr. Goggs, down the steps, up the passage, and into the garden, where he ran against the shoeblack, who was carrying two buckets full of savory wash, intended for the evening refreshment of Mr. Goggs's pig. But the pig lost his tea. The dog rolled over Mr. Goggs, Mr. Goggs rolled over the shoeblack, and the shoeblack rolled over the buckets of wash; and, when Tom Pippin and the boys arrived upon the scene, the head-master of Dumplington Grammar-School was lying on the ground, surrounded by a pool of something which scarcely differed in appearance from the hashed mutton served out twice a week to his pupils, while the dog was shaking the reverend gentleman's coat-collar between his teeth, and looking as if it would afford him inexpressible pleasure to shake his windpipe as well.

Tom instantly called him off, put on his company manners, and apologized. "Upon my word, sir," he began, "I'm doosid sorry—I am, indeed. Come away, Grab. I hope he has not—aw—hurt you."

Mr. Goggs endeavored to explain, between his gasps for breath, that it is not nice to be soused with pigs' wash, or pinned down, in the middle of your own garden, by a great brute as big as a heifer. He then asked Tom Pippin his business, and flatly refused, without any reservation, to permit the lads to dine with him. "Certainly not, sir," he said. "Teasel is a day boy, and may do as his father pleases; but I should not think of allowing any indulgence to so unsatisfactory a boy as Nightshade; and as for Northcote, he is a disgrace to the school. Indeed, I have serious thoughts of expelling him."

"Hooray!" cried Harry, who was looking on with half a dozen other fellows, from the garden door.

"Boys, go away directly!" shouted Mr. Goggs; "you are all out of bounds." And the reverend gentleman made as though he would pursue them. But Tom Pippin telegraphed a private signal to Grab, who still waited for orders beside him; and the dog put himself at once into a playful attitude which induced the schoolmaster to stay quietly where he was.

"Then—aw—you won't—aw—let them come?" said Tom, urging a last appeal. "Aw, sorry for that. Hear there's a meeting at the town hall to-night. I'm

—aw—fond of meetings. Boys and I were thinking of aw looking in for half an hour."

"I fear, sir," said Mr. Goggs, as portentously as if he were pronouncing some fellow-creature's final doom, "I fear that their hearts are not yet sufficiently under the influence of grace to enable them to profit by any godly exercise."

"Aw," said Tom, apologetically, I didn't know." And then he added, out of good-natured consideration for the boys' noses at tea-time, "Aw, don't presume to advise, but aw—think you'll be more comfortable if I go away, and leave you to—aw—change your things." Tom felt perfectly certain, by the very color of the man's linen, that he would sit down to table just as he was, pigs' wash and all. And so he did.

"Well," said Tom to his young friends, as he passed through the schoolroom again, "I knew that schoolmasters were very often brutes, but I did think they were gentlemen. Good-by, Harry. If that fellow touches you again, Grab shall throttle him. Come along with me, Frank, and I'll give you some food to bring back to these poor boys for supper. I am sure they won't be able to eat any tea, if that nasty man doesn't change his coat."

The nasty man's wrath, when he sat down in his nastiness, was a thing terrible to behold. Even cutlets and tomato-sauce failed to stroke him down. He was by habit an unclean feeder, was Mr. Goggs; flinging himself furiously upon his plate, as if he would slaughter afresh, with angry knife and fork, the beast which had been sacrificed that it might minister to his desires. He gobbled much, did Mr. Goggs, making many noises

with his palate as he disposed of his food. For economy's sake he was denied a napkin ; so that the exte-
rior surface of his lips bore perpetually a marginal
reference to the work which was going on within. He
talked, and even drank, with his mouth full, quaffing
beer after apple-tart and sipping it after salmon. When
his appetite was appeased, he paraded with undue publicity his toothpick, and was at little pains to conceal
within decent limits the outward and visible symptoms
of a weak digestion. It is very vulgar to describe
such disgusting things, is it not, dear reader? A man
must have a thoroughly plebeian mind to think of anything so low. Of course he must. But what about
those aristocratically-minded people who don't *describe*
such disgusting things, but *do* them? do them unblushingly every day, in the face of their wives, their daughters, their pupils, or their friends? You open your
eyes with wonder at your dear boy's manners, when he
comes home for his first holidays ; but you would not
believe, if any one declared it to you, that he has
learned how to eat and drink like a pig from nobody
on earth except the gentlemanly farmer of youths to
whose establishment you have sent him to have his
mind improved.

"Northcote," said Mr. Goggs, looking up for a
moment from his dainty dish, "who was that person
that came in just now?"

"What person, sir?" returned Harry, who never
spoke otherwise than impudently to his distant cousin,
if he remembered it in time.

"You know very well!" sputtered Mr. Goggs, with
two great flakes of a Spanish onion dangling out of his

mouth. "The person that brought in that wild beast of a dog. I'll have him shot next time he comes!"

"Have him shot, sir! What, Mr. Pippin, sir?" exclaimed Harry, putting on a look of the deepest concern, as if he were trembling for his friend's life.

"Leave the room, sir!" roared Mr. Goggs, who had by this time gathered up and swallowed the flakes of onion. "And you will understand that I distinctly forbid Mr. Pippin or any other friend of yours to enter my schoolroom again."

"Yes, sir," said Harry, well pleased to escape from the smell of the nasty man's coat twenty minutes before any of his less favored schoolfellows.

The nasty man, however, changed his coat, and made himself look moderately respectable, before he took the chair at the missionary meeting in the town hall. Mrs. Goggs was too unwell to accompany him, so she remained at home and read a tract on the conversion of a Hottentot prince to some boys in the sickroom. What a motherly woman she was! The little fellows had tasted nothing but gruel for three days at least, and were crying aloud for chops and a glass of beer. But she had the wisdom to resist their entreaties, knowing far better than they did what was good for them. And when the tract was finished, and she had offered up a prayer, she collected such odd threepenny pieces as they had in their pockets, and put them by for the missionaries. A most inestimable woman was Mrs. Goggs.

The meeting was a decided success. Ministers of all denominations were present, eager to testify their interest in the common cause. The Rev. Ebenezer

Slimes was there, his sallow whitewashed countenance wearing that peculiar look of pious resignation which befitted one who, to all appearance, had nothing very valuable to resign. Hymns were sung, minutes read, and various preliminary business transacted; while half a dozen gentlemen, in suits of shining threadbare black, with a Bible prominently displayed in one pocket, and a ticket of leave carefully concealed in the other, walked about the room distributing portraits of piebald negroes digging holes under a palm-tree, or chiefs with feathers in their heads, falling down to stocks and stones. It would be unfair to inquire too diligently what they took from the audience in exchange. We may content ourselves with the assurance that whatever trifle this or that middle-aged lady may afterwards have missed, it was something which it was good for her soul's health to lose; and that the pious purloiner thereof would never have abstracted it, unless for the sake of weaning its owner's affections from earthly things.

This profitable business over, the deputation from the parent society entertained the company with select and refined anecdotes of negro life which were not even founded on fact, and exhorted them with painful eloquence to pursue what certainly never was, and we trust never will be, the way to glory. Then the Rev. Ebenezer Slimes was called upon by his dear brother in the chair to move the first resolution: "That this meeting, taking into consideration the overwhelming importance of missionary work abroad, do consider that missionary work abroad is a matter of the most overwhelming importance." (Hear, hear.) The reverend gentleman spoke in chaste and highly grammatical English for three-quarters of an hour, and his resolution was carried unanimously.

Will any one explain to me what comes of all the resolutions that are passed? Some of them look very terrible on paper, but what happens afterwards? Does the enthusiastic multitude rush off bodily, to carry butcher's meat to a cannibal, or convert a Jew? Is any mortal man one halfpenny the better, or one halfpenny the worse, because the right reverend chairman moved the adoption of the report, and the report was adopted accordingly?

At the termination of these edifying proceedings Mr. Goggs retired, with the deputation and the Rev. Ebenezer Slimes, to the inn in Slipper Lane kept by the last-named gentleman's wife's cousin. Here they provoked one another to piety over frequently replenished cups of whatever stimulating beverage was best adapted for the purpose, and refreshed each other's minds with godly conversation till twelve o'clock. About this period Mr. Slimes became so very drunk, and the deputation's anecdotes grew so extremely coarse, that Mr. Goggs supplicated a blessing upon their mutual labors, and walked home with the greatest amount of perpendicularity to the pavement which it was convenient to maintain.

Meanwhile, Tom Pippin also indulged in a little quiet dissipation, after a more worldly and carnal sort. Cheated out of his fun with the boys, he invited himself to dinner in the Close, at the house of his old friends Dr. and Miss Stuart.

"Just in time," said the doctor. "We have young

Crookleigh staying with us, and Lady Maria. The lad
comes to me now and then, you know, to be looked
after, and his sister likes to keep him company. I am
afraid he is in a very bad way; but she is wonderfully
improved, both in mind and body. I can't think,
Tom, why you don't go in for her."

"I have need to do something or other with myself," answered Tom, "for I am in a desperate mess,
and that's the truth. Three blessed hours this day
have I been going into accounts with that fellow Teasel,
and it is perfectly awful to think of the amount I owe.
And by Jove, as far as I can make out, *he* has got himself,
by some speculation or other, into a worse hobble still."

"Tell the earl," suggested Dr. Stuart.

"Tell the——any one else you like," said Tom.
"The whole object of his venerable life is to save up
every pound he can lay hands on for young Russet;
and if I were to beg for it I don't believe he would
chuck me half a crown."

"Then come up into my room and wash your hands,
old fellow, for I see that you have got nothing to
change; and when we have sent Crookleigh to bed,
and drunk a bottle of claret, you shall have the drawing-room all to yourself, and propose to Lady Maria."

While Tom's roast beef was cooling on his plate, because he could not get any mustard to eat with it, he
had ample leisure to judge for himself how far Lady
Maria's personal appearance had improved. For some
reason hitherto unexplained, it is vulgar to let the
mustard-pot stand upon the table; and, as it is simply
impossible to touch beef without it, one is forced to
postpone one's dinner until every vegetable dish in the

room has been handed round, and the footman, purely
as an after-thought, fetches the desired stimulant from
the sideboard. But after contemplating Lady Maria's
countenance steadily for a minute and a half, Tom
wanted something more than mustard to make his beef
go down. He had no appetite for anything. She was
hideous beyond all belief. Tom felt quite certain he
could never make up his mind to it ; so he drank a glass
of sherry, and let his eyes wander across the table no
more.

At nine o'clock, poor young Crookleigh was sent to
bed, looking very much as if he would never have the
strength to get up again. At half-past nine the doctor
was summoned to attend a patient ; and Lady Maria,
Miss Stuart, and Tom were left to spend the evening
by themselves. Miss Stuart, who was as innocent as a
baby of all matrimonial schemings, quitted the drawing-
room as soon as she had drunk a cup of tea, and went
up-stairs to discharge some kindly office for Lord Crookleigh. So the two "young people" were in the room
together ; and Tom kept on wondering to himself
whether he should do it then and there, or let it alone.

At last he did it. In spite of his high spirits with the
boys in the afternoon, Tom was involved to an extent
which would have driven many and many a man to
absolute despair. What could he do? Edith was all
very well, but it was not possible to live either with or
without her for nothing. And Tom had less than
nothing. Fifty thousand pounds less than nothing.
Whereas, if he could only bring himself to say five words
to Lady Maria, he would have a hundred thousand a
year. Crookleigh might perhaps live a couple of months.

The duke had not another relation in the world.   And Tom Pippin, just now, through his silly old uncle's fault, the poorest beggar in Dumplingshire, would send two members to Parliament, and divide the county with the earl.

"It's all my eye to talk about love," said Tom to himself; "so here goes."

"Maria, dear Maria," he said, sitting down beside her, but *not* possessing himself of her moist hand. "Maria, dear Maria! I do—aw—love you so!"

"Come, come, Tom, I may be half a fool, but I know better than that!" said Lady Maria, giggling, and making faces like an ape.

"Indeed I do, Maria! I have—aw—loved you from your—aw—infancy."

"My infancy!" roared Lady Maria. "Really, Tom, that is rather too good! My infancy! Ah, I was a lovely infant, Tom, wasn't I? Pity I didn't grow up an infant, Tom. I might have been lovely still." And here she grinned at him after a fashion which frightened Tom pretty nearly out of his wits, and made him jump off the sofa, and put the tea-table between him and his love.

"Don't run away, Tom," began Lady Maria again. "You ought to come and kiss me, Tom, and squeeze my hand. It is a nice hand, Tom. Come and feel."

Poor Tom did not know what on earth to do. He was wholly unprepared for such a reception. The little speeches that he had made up over his wine were framed upon the most conventional model, and proved utterly inapplicable to so eccentric a wooing. So he sat on the edge of his chair at the other side of the table, staring with a horrible fascination into the lady's face, and ready to bolt out of the house in case her idiocy should take a violent turn.

"You won't come and kiss me, Tom?" said Lady Maria. "Well, I must say that's rather hard. Nobody ever has kissed me. People always said I was too ugly. But I did think, when any young man came and told me he had loved me from my infancy, that I should get a kiss then. Do you know, Tom, I have a very great mind to come across and kiss *you?*"

"If you move from your seat, Tom, I will," she continued, seeing that Tom was pushing back his chair. "Why don't you ask me for my photograph, Tom, or a lock of my golden hair? I am afraid the stupid people forgot to have my likeness taken in my infancy, Tom, when you first began to love me."

"Maria," faltered Tom, finding some sort of voice at last, "I am afraid you have—aw—misunderstood me."

"Why, you are never going to back out of it, Tom?" she returned. "Surely it is a *bona fide* offer of marriage, isn't it? Mr. Thomas Pippin, of Ribstone Court, to the amiable and attractive Lady Maria Bent, only daughter of the Duke of Dumplingshire. No, no, Tom! I sha'n't let you off now, you know."

"It is a vewy—aw—serious matter," observed Tom, sententiously. "Too serious for joking, Maria."

"I am not joking, Tom," she returned, leaning across the table and looking at him, something less hideously than before. "I am very much in earnest. And I will tell you a little secret, Tom. You don't love me one bit, Tom; you know you don't. You only want my money. Now, I *do* love *you*—love you

with all my heart and soul—love you as only a woman
can love—as only an ugly misshapen woman can love,
who can never get her love back again, and must needs
love enough for two. You don't know what love
means, Tom. You don't even love your Edith as she
deserves to be loved, or you would never come to me
like this. Go back to her, Tom, and love her better,
and tell her that the poor ungainly idiot had more
sense for once than the handsome, popular man of
fashion. Tell her that the cripple, with coarse carroty
hair, loved Tom Pippin with a love so true, that when
she had him at her feet, and might take him if she
would, she saved him from his own folly, and forbore
to chain him for life to a miserable object, who could
only bring him into contempt with all the world. Tell
her this, Tom; and tell her also, if you will, that
whatever little money the idiot may possess shall be
poured into her lap on her bridal morning, that he
whom the idiot has dared to love may be happy and
free.''

"Ah, Maria," said Tom, half crying as he spoke,
"it is something more than a 'little money' that will
make me happy and free. I am simply ruined; and
there is no more chance of my marrying Edith than
of my marrying Queen Anne."

"And so, as a last resource, you want to marry me,"
said Lady Maria. "Well, that is kind of you, Tom.
But what do you mean by 'ruined'? How much do
you suppose you owe?"

"Fifty thousand at the very least; and, what is
more, it must be raised immediately. I am mixed up
with a set of fellows here who will bring me to hope-

less grief if I don't get clear of them at once.   There
is only one way to do it, Maria.   You say that you
love me.   I'll take my oath that I love *you*.   Of course
I want your money; but I want you too.   Let us
make a match of it.   It's a sort of thing that people—
aw—do every day."

"I can't think why you don't go to your uncle,
Tom.   The money would not be so very much to
him."

"Might as well go to the moon," said Tom.   "I
know him better than you do.   Come, say yes, Maria,
and make me happy."

"If I thought it would make you happy, I would
say yes fifty times over," answered she.   "Or if I
knew for certain that there was no other way of raising the money, I would say the same."

"There is no other way," said Tom.   "The duke
would clear me directly if I married you.   He and
my uncle tried it on, don't you recollect, ever so long
ago?"

"Well, Tom, I think you are quite wrong; but it
shall be as you wish.   Only, please understand that you
are perfectly and entirely free.   Free to throw me over,
free to go back to Edith, free at any time to take my
money and leave me out in the cold.   So now good-
night; and remember that the idiot won't reproach you
by a single word if you change your mind to-morrow."

"I've done it," said Tom, meeting Dr. Stuart at the
hall door, and looking very much as if he were going
to be hung in the morning.

"No, have you, really?" said the doctor.   "Come
back and tell me all about it over a glass of whisky."

"Not to-night, thank you." And then Tom went off to his hotel.

When he had rung the coffee-room bell for the invigorating brandy-and-soda, without which no young man of well-regulated mind ever thinks of going to bed, Boots appeared behind the waiter; not to bring a pair of nasty buff slippers, into which three generations of nasty travelers had thrust their nasty feet—for Tom had his own ideas of comfort, as well as of cleanliness, and would sooner have sat all night in his high-lows—but to convey the mournful intelligence that Grab was missing. The dog had slipped out of the yard about ten o'clock; while Boots was seeing of a gent drive away; and he had not returned. Boots had been held in a measure responsible for the creature's safety; and, with many signs of penitence, he begged to be informed, first, whether his master had seen him anywhere about; secondly, whether he should tell the police; and thirdly, whether Mr. Pippin knew of any place where such another dog could be procured, in case he turned out to be irretrievably lost.

"Bless your heart," said Tom, "don't alarm yourself. He's all right. If you sleep as sound to-night as he will, you'll be pretty fresh in the morning. Trust Grab to find himself a bed, and supper, too."

Grab had indeed found for himself both bed and supper. When he gained his liberty at ten o'clock— for, to say the truth, Boots with his kind attentions had been rather an anxiety to him—the dog visited first the chief public buildings of the town, then thoroughly "did" the precincts of the cathedral, and finally determined, before retiring to rest, to earn another shake of his huge paw, and another boisterous hug round his

shaggy neck, from his dear young master, Harry Northcote. Grab's notions about school-hours were not perhaps clearly defined; but, as he had never appeared
upon the playground yet without having half a dozen
arms flung affectionately round him, and more than one
pair of small legs set astride across his back, he drew
the sagacious and very doggish conclusion that games
went on perpetually. For once, however, he found the
green in front of the schoolroom deserted. Not a single merry shout responded to the wagging of his tail,
though the full moon lit up the frosted grass so bril-
liantly that Grab could not for the life of him comprehend why it was not daytime, and why the boys did
not come out and play. A wicket or two lay scattered
about, and a white flannel jacket was stiffening in the
cold. Grab carried them one by one to the top of the
steps, down which his young friends had so often rushed
to caress him. Perhaps he thought, dear dog, that he
would get some little fellow out of a row, by bringing
in the jacket which he had been "so abominably and
disgracefully careless as to leave outside—totally against
the rules of the school." If so, he was mistaken, for
the crime had been discovered in the moonlight, and
Mrs. Goggs, spying out from her bedroom window, had
long ago sworn a saintly oath that in the morning an
example should be made. When he had rubbed his
head in the jacket, as the next best thing to embracing
its owner, Grab thumped the schoolroom door with his
tail, scratched at the crevices underneath, shook the
handle with his paws, grew sorrowful and whined, grew
indignant and growled, grew angry and barked, and
then pricked up his ears and stood erect, listening for

the repetition of a low clear whistle, which could proceed from no other mouth than that of his very particular friend.

Now it happened that the good things which Tom
Pippin sent down to the schoolroom by Frank Teasel's
hands had arrived too late to allow of their being consumed before bedtime. The boys resolved, therefore,
to take the opportunity, while Mr. Goggs was out of
the way, to smuggle the various provisions up-stairs,
and to hold a feast, at some convenient hour of the
night, in one of the bedrooms. The feast, however,
must of necessity be postponed until the reverend gentleman's return, because he was perfectly certain to
sneak up the back staircase without his boots, and to
listen at each bedroom door as he passed to his own
sacred chamber; so that it would not be safe to begin
banqueting until he had been heard to lock himself in
for the night. In accordance with the judicious cus-
tom of all pettifogging schools, the boys at Dumplington were sent to bed at half-past eight o'clock—partly
to save the expense of gas, and partly to save masters
the trouble of looking after the farm any longer. The
wisdom of this arrangement is manifest. It being
utterly impossible for any boy, from twelve to sixteen
or so, to go to sleep at such an hour, he lies awake,
with his bright imagination hard at work to discover
the pleasantest mode of getting through the time, and
with full liberty to think, act, or say just whatever his
bright imagination may suggest to him. "Thank
goodness!" says the farmer, as he sits down to his
Saturday Review while the supper is being laid, "I'm
well rid of them all for to-night, at any rate!" "Yes,

my love," says the farmer's wife; "and think of the
pounds we save, by putting out the fire and the gas so
nice and early! Besides, if they sat up late, we should
have to give them bread and cheese, you know." It
might be worth your while, my dear Mrs. Deemon, if
you could only look a little further ahead; it might be
worth your while in the end to give them not bread
and cheese only, but a good big slice of cold roast
beef, and a hunch of cake besides. You may save
your gas, and your husband may shirk his responsibility;
and even yet you may have something extra to pay. We
will hope that your boys are heavenly boys, and can be
trusted to lie awake for an hour and a half before any
one else ever dreams of going to bed, with no check
upon them, and with nothing to do. But, if they should
chance to be common earthly boys, then, for all the
mischief that is done in that hour and a half, whatever
it may be—for the bad words spoken, the poisonous
stories told, the evil lessons taught, the bullying, practiced simply to pass away the time,—for all this you
will have to give account, and a pretty reckoning it
will be. Your only chance lies in letting the boys do
just the very thing which you will not let them do at
any price—kick up a jolly good row. Where there is
noise, there is safety. If the mere suspicion should
arise of a bolstering-match, or a feast spread on one of
the beds, or any such dangerous breach of the peace,
Mr. Deemon would rush up-stairs with weapons, and
his wife stand aghast with horror. *That* would soil
the sheets, and make a mess, and give the servants
trouble. The room would have to be scrubbed again
before any parents could be shown over it; counter-

panes would have to go to the wash, and pillow-cases to be mended. Boys who could perpetrate such an outrage would merit to be caned all round, and the ringleaders would narrowly escape expulsion. But so long as they go quietly to bed, and let you save your coals and gas, what do you care how much harm may happen to them? So grin away, Mr. Deemon, over your *Saturday Review;* and cast up your weekly profits, Mrs. Deemon, with complacent face; and then fall to, and eat your supper, and never mind the hungry stomachs up stairs. There is nobody to tell. Boy-farming is the safest possible trade. Only the boys know anything of its secrets; and if *they* say a word, bless you, they won't be believed.

On this particular Friday night, in this special month of November, things were in training for as merry a feast as starving schoolboys could desire. There was an enormous veal-and-ham pie, which had been "made to order" for somebody else, but which the pastrycook had generously yielded up to Tom Pippin, to the immense gratification, no doubt, of the individual who had ordered it. Then there were cakes and tarts and sausage-rolls, and a dozen bottles of beer (oh, naughty Tom!), and oceans of sweets to be sucked quietly in bed; and finally, what the young revelers would appreciate more than anything else, some *real good* bread and cheese. Bread almost hot, in dear little twopenny cottage loaves; and cheese which tasted of cheese, and not of yellow soap, as did the lumps of sickly-looking stuff served out as a treat on Sunday night for supper—which lumps the boys always declared to be "second-hand," and to have been pre-

viously suspended on wire in Mrs. Goggs's numerous
mousetraps.   Mrs. Goggs was much afflicted with mice.
She had more than once essayed to keep a cat; but the
boys paid such marked attentions to the animal, in
recognition of its mistress's spite against themselves,
that the situation became known throughout the town
as untenable, and no cat would remain in the house on
any terms.

The dormitory in which these preparations had been
made was a long room running right across the house,
with one window placed over the front door and another looking into the back garden.   On this particular
moonlight night there could be no difficulty, therefore,
in watching the schoolmaster's approach several hundred yards before he reached the door; but the schoolmaster would not come.   At half-past ten the boys lost
patience, and divided the spoil; eating the pie, which
was inconveniently full of gravy, out of their respective soap-dishes, and proving, by their successful use
of primitive expedients, that forks and spoons are the
mere superfluities of an extravagant age.   They were
still hard at it, passing broken tooth-mugs full of beer
from bed to bed, "swopping" sausage-rolls for tarts,
or cake for cheese, and making a great deal more noise
than was safe, even in their master's absence,—when
Harry Northcote, who slept against the window, but
who had been too much engaged of late to look out of
it, heard first a whine, and then a growl, and then a
bark, which could proceed from no other mouth than
that of his very particular friend.

"By Jove!" he cried, springing out of bed, "there's
old Grab sitting on the steps by the schoolroom door!"

"*So* there is!" exclaimed half a dozen other fellows, flocking in their night-shirts to the window, while Harry whistled softly to his favorite, through a broken pane of glass. "*So* there is. Let's shy him down some grub!"

"Oh, yes, *do* let's!" said a fat, good-natured youth from the other end of the room, who had been too lazy to turn out. "Bags I giving him my tarts. I don't want 'em."

"You ass, Punch!" said Harry. "As if a dog would eat tarts! Look here, who's got any pie left? Hanged if mine isn't all gone."

"Here you are, Harry," said two or three of the small boys, who would have given up their whole share to their friend, even if he had not wanted it for Grab.

So a liberal contribution was made, and a highly miscellaneous meal was tied up in a towel, for the dear dog's supper. A pocket-handkerchief had been proffered for the purpose, but it was getting towards the end of the week, and Harry indignantly asked the owner how he would like it himself, and whether he thought that a dog hadn't got any feelings.

The next question was, how to get the food downstairs. If the bundle were fastened up tight enough to prevent the scraps from tumbling out when thrown from the window, could the dog be trusted to untie it? Harry believed he could; but it was impossible to say. Could even such teeth as *his* penetrate one of Mrs. Goggs's serviceable towels? That, again, was doubtful. "Well," said Harry, jumping up at last, and putting on his trousers, "I don't care a hang! I've been licked twice to-day, and I've got more than two

thousand lines to show up on Monday; and now I'll
just give that beast something to spite me for!" So
saying, he opened the window, called Grab, who came
bounding over a wall about six feet high, instructed
him by mystic signs to lie down quietly at the front
door, and then crept as softly as possible down the
creaking stairs, bundle in hand.

He had scarcely turned the handle of the door when
Grab pushed himself in, rushed upon him with dem-
onstrations of the wildest joy, licked his hands, his
feet, and his neck, burrowed with his cold nose into
the boy's open chest, tickling poor Harry to such an
extent that he rolled right over with laughter, and altogether took the meanest advantage of the accident
which had placed his young master for once completely
in his power. Turn which way he would, Harry could
not get rid of him. The more he wriggled about, the
more fresh places the animal found out to torment him
in; till the boy determined at last that his best chance
lay in keeping quiet, and resigning himself patiently
to the dog's caresses, while he freed his arm from
the pressure of his assailant's huge paw, and un-
fastened the bundle of provisions. Then Grab—for
he was but a dog after all — sniffed at the good
things, left his young master alone, and straightway
devoured his supper; with but little more speed,
and infinitely less noise and commotion, than Mr.
Goggs was wont to make over his French beans or
asparagus.

Harry was just gathering up the broken scraps in the
moonlight, and wondering within himself, first, why
Mrs. Goggs did not come out of her room and catch

him; secondly, how on earth he should fetch the dog some water without being followed up-stairs; and, thirdly, how he might best prevail upon Grab to go back to the inn: when he espied the clumsy figure of the schoolmaster staggering across the green. Like a dear good dog as he was, Grab suffered himself to be seized by the collar and pushed without ceremony outside the door; but Harry had scarcely time to reach his bed in safety when the Rev. Goggs, with a somewhat unsteady method of progression, advanced to the garden gate. Advanced, but speedily retired; for Grab had his eye upon him; and, if the schoolmaster had dared to come inside the gateway, Grab would have had his paw upon him too. Mr. Goggs was not the sort of man to place his life or even his limbs in danger. "I must let myself in through the back door," muttered that pious farmer of boys; "and, if I don't have that brute's throat cut in the morning, my name isn't Hezekiah Goggs." That brute, however, who appeared to consider that the schoolmaster had been specially intrusted to his charge by Harry and Tom, paid Mr. Goggs the compliment to spring over the playground wall, and to follow him to the back-garden gate, which the reverend gentleman was so far fuddled, after his missionary dissipations, as to slam carelessly behind him, and leave ajar. Grab pushed it open, howled in the very exuberance of his great joy, chased his enemy over paths and cabbage-stumps and beds of celery, and was in the act of dragging him backwards by the tail of his coat, when Mr. Goggs, recalling in his dire extremity the elasticities of his youth, cleared the low paling which served his pig for a palace

boundary, and bolted clean into the sty, barring the
door behind him.

Fifteen boys from their bedroom window roaring
with delight; four servant-maids from their cold attic,
shivering, yet clapping their hands for glee; one
wretched shoeblack, from his straw bed in the stable-
loft, glorying over the stingy taskmaster who had upset
him in the afternoon; and one invalid wife, with
nerves unstrung, aroused out of her first delicious
sleep, wherein she had contemplated troops of starving
children fed from her bosom with a tender mother's
care: all these were spectators of the scene. Mr.
Goggs seemed determined to collect as many spectators upon the ground as possible; for he raised, from
his savory resting-place, repeated shrieks of murder, to
which the pig responded with indignant grunts and the
dog with angry barkings. Could nothing be done to
save him? The invalid wife with nerves unstrung
resolved at last that an effort should be made. The
ushers were none of them sleeping in the house; she
would call to her assistance some of the bigger boys—
bound to help her by every tie of loyalty—specially
bound to show their gratitude for favors recently vouchsafed. Had she not given Crawford two helpings of
suet-pudding that very day? Had she not, on summer
evenings, indulged the boys so far as to allow them to
come into her garden and water the vegetables and
flowers, saving their dear master about ten shillings a
week thereby? Had she not also, when tired to death
of playing croquet with her lord, who held his mallet
as a plowman holds a spoon, and cheated frightfully,—had not she permitted some of the boys to vary

the monotony of the game by sitting up late and playing with her, giving them a bunch of out-door grapes
and half a glass of home-made ginger wine for supper?
Had she not paid them the distinguished honor, again
and again, of sending them up into the town, just as
they were going to begin cricket or football, to buy
her sixpennyworth of tape at some cheap shop for five-
pence farthing, or bargain with the butcher to let her
have some unusually dainty morsel, wherewith to make
a pie for the young gentlemen, at half price? Surely
the young gentlemen were not so destitute of human
feelings as to be unmindful of benefits such as these.
She robed herself, therefore, and descended the stairs;
constitutionally unable, however, even when time was
so exceeding precious, to resist the temptation of listening at the bedroom door. "I wish they would not
all talk at once!" sighed the ill-used woman at last.
"I really can't hear a word they say." Then she
knocked for admittance; and the boys, waiting for a
moment to hear the knock repeated, scuttled away—
flying headlong into the first unoccupied bed that happened to stand near, and not very particular whether
it were occupied or not, if only the rightful tenant
were small enough to afford them shelter and conceal-
ment in his narrow crib.

"Crawford," she began—under no circumstances
had she ever been known to address a boy by his
Christian name—"Crawford, I shall not this time
report you, as captain of this dormitory, for the dis-
graceful noise which I heard on entering the room."

"Thank you, ma'am," said Crawford.

"Because I wish you, and two or three of the elder

boys, instantly to put on your things, and go down into
the garden to help Mr. Goggs, who is unfortunately
shut up in the—the—outhouse."

"Pig-sty, ma'am," said Crawford.

"Well, never mind where it is. I desire that you,
and Vyvyan, and Melvill will go and drive away that
dreadful dog immediately."

"Please 'em, there isn't a fellow in the school that
would dare go near him," urged Crawford, who was
about the pluckiest boy that ever lived, and would
have faced a lion and a bear in defense of any one else
but his beloved master.

"I'll go, ma'am," said Harry, who thought the joke
had now gone far enough. "It's only Grab. He'll
come away directly, if I run down and catch hold of
him."

In less than half a minute after the amiable matron
had made herself scarce, Harry was in the garden, with
his arm flung round his favorite's neck, coaxing him to
leave his prey; while Mr. Goggs, kneeling with damp
shins upon his bed of filth, and hugging the pig affectionately with both his arms, was coaxing the companion of his captivity to turn his snout in the other
direction, and not to allay the irritation of his skin by
rubbing his head caressingly up and down his master's
waistcoat.

By this time the whole house had been made aware
of the calamity which had befallen its chief. Boys had
crept up-stairs from Crawford's room to telegraph the
glad tidings to the less wakeful youths above. Every
window was thronged with eager faces, peering into the
moonlit garden. Every landing on the staircase was

crowded with boys in white, their teeth chattering as they cheered, unmindful of the cold November night, unmindful of bare legs and naked throats, if only they might catch one glimpse of Goggs before Grab had let him go. But among all that joyous company, none were so ecstatic in their glee as the three sons of Mr. Goggs's own body begotten.

"Hooray!" cried Bobby. "Pa's in the pig-sty! Hope he'll never get out again. Hooray!" Then he ran into the small boys' room to tell his younger brothers, who were scarcely yet *bona fide* members of the academy, passing an amphibious existence between the schoolroom and the nursery, being thumped by the usher in the morning for pronouncing Latin like French, and slapped by their sisters' governess in the afternoon for pronouncing French like Latin.

"Goggs minor," said Bobby, "get up as quick as you can, and wake Minimus. Here's such a lark. Pa's in the pig-sty!"

"Goggs minimus," said Freddy, as soon as he had realized the importance of the news; "Goggs minimus! can't you hear? Jump up directly. Pa's in the pig-sty! Hooray!"

"Hooray!" echoed little Johnny, tottering drowsily to the window. "Oh, I do so *wish* the pig would gobble him up—I do, I do, I *do!*"

But thanks to Harry's protection, pa was now a free man. And when he saw that the boy had the animal so completely under control, pa became suddenly a courageous man, and then a furiously angry man.

"Hold him, Northcote!" he shouted; "hold him tight, while I get a big stone, and dash his brains out!"

9

"No, sir!" pleaded Harry.   "He'll kill you if you
touch him—really he will!"

But Mr. Goggs was long past the influence of persua-
sion.   Mad with rage, he tore up a couple of enormous
stones from some rock-work close by, and hurled them
one after another at the dog and the boy together, as
if it were a matter of perfect indifference to him which
of the two he brained.   Of course he missed them both
by about a yard and a half, being as clumsy a shot as
you would meet in a day's journey; but Harry did not
choose to stand still and be shied at by such a lunatic
again.   Restraining Grab, therefore, by numerous en-
dearments from flying at the lunatic's throat, he led the
creature across the cabbage-stumps and through the
garden gate, which Mr. Goggs effectually this time shut
behind them by dashing against it a stone something
smaller than his own misshapen head.   This was too
much for Harry.   The man was becoming dangerous,
and Grabb should not be killed, if he could help it, before his very eyes.   The dog, clearly, would not go
home without him; therefore he would see the dog
home.   He would break any amount of school rules,
and stand his chance of expulsion itself, rather than see
his darling Grab slaughtered in cold blood upon the
doorstep.   So they started off together, unpursued by
Mr. Goggs, who could not get through his shattered door;
and a merry scamper they had, across the green, and
down three or four streets, and into the Red Lion yard.

"You sha'n't go back to-night, boy," said Tom
Pippin, when he had embraced his favorite, and heard
his young friend's story.

"Oh, but, Tom, I must indeed," urged Harry.   "I

shall get into such an awful row. Besides, Goggs will come and fetch me."

"He had better," said Tom. "He shall have something handsome to carry back with him; but he sha'n't have *you*. By Jove, I would not trust you in that brute's clutches to-night for any money. I'll owe him one for trying to murder my dear dog; but I won't give him the chance of doing you a mischief. No, no, you shall have a bed here."

Tom Pippin always had his own way, so Harry slept at the Red Lion; and Mr. Goggs was far too frantic in his wrath to bother himself that night with any inquiries whether Northcote had returned to his dormitory or no.

In the morning Tom got up at the unwonted hour of seven, and walked with Harry back to school. "I'll just wait a minute outside," he said, as the boys assembled at the half-hour, and work, such as it was, began. "I'll condescend for once to listen at the door—a thing I wouldn't do for anybody else, Master Harry, any more than I'd get up at seven. And, if that beggar dares to lay a finger on you, by George he shall be a mummy before breakfast-time!"

But Tom need not have troubled himself either to get up at seven, or to utter threats, or to listen at the door. Mr. Goggs did not appear in school on that day or on the next. His nerves, like those of his invalid wife, were wholly unstrung. His combined experiences of Mr. Teasel in the study, of Grab in the garden, and of the pig in the sty, had been too much for him, and for two entire days he was confined to his room. On the third day he resumed the management of the farm;

but he had been chastened by adversity, and tried in
the furnace of affliction. Subdued and sad, he resolved
to fight no more, but to make peace with his enemies
all round. Grab should be pardoned for his assaults;
Harry Northcote and his friend, who had been robbed
of their oranges and brawn, should receive their shilling
apiece; and Mr. Teasel should have his apology.

"Northcote," said Mr. Goggs, for not even when
chastened by adversity could the man do a straightfor-
ward action,—"Northcote, here is a shilling for you,
as a reward for your assistance in the garden. And
who was the other boy whom Mrs. Goggs sent down to
help you with the dog? Freeland, was it not?"

"No, sir," answered Harry, thunderstruck at his
relative's unheard-of munificence. "There was no
other boy, sir."

"Ah, well, I said Freeland, so I will not disappoint
him. Freeland, here is your shilling." And thus it
was that the minister of religion trained up children in
the way in which it is to be devoutly hoped that they
did not go, and conscientiously fulfilled the first half
of the stern conditions imposed by Mr. Teasel.

The other half, however, of his unpalatable duty had
yet to be discharged. By this time Mr. Teasel must
have returned to Dumplington, from the little trip-to-
town-on-business in which Mrs. Teasel had accompanied him. There had been a certain amount of
significance in the lawyer's intimation that his wife
would share his journey. Very few of his journeys,
whether on business or pleasure, did his faithful partner
share. Mr. Teasel was a popular man, and a highly
respectable man, in spite of the mystery which shrouded

his professional pursuits from the vulgar gaze and baffled the gossipings even of a Cathedral town. But, for all that, Mr. Teasel was a villain, inasmuch as he behaved badly to his wife. By this it is not meant that he went about with wives appertaining to other people. His bad behavior amounted to nothing more than a trifling misapprehension of liabilities incurred. He simply neglected the poor woman, left her alone, took his holidays without her, and claimed the right to enjoy perpetually all bachelor immunities from household care, looking to his wife for an ungrudging supply of household comforts whenever it suited his convenience to remain at home. There are plenty of such men, and they seem to me to be wholly without an excuse for their villainy. The unmarried wretch, moping by his solitary fireside, rewards himself for his wretchedness overnight by rambling on the morrow whithersoever he will. He sets the delights of companionship against the untold joys of liberty, and says to himself that he is happier if he so abide. But, if he marries, let it be for better for worse. Let him stick loyally to his wife, as he would have his wife stick loyally to him. He has no right to play the bachelor just when it pleases him. He has no business to run down for a fortnight to the seaside and leave his wife to keep house at home. He is a villain if he dines out every day for a month, because his wife has got a baby. Of course she declares she likes it, and wishes him to go, and is far happier to be left alone, and to feel satisfied that he will get a good dinner with his friends elsewhere. Women always say these things; and men, knowing nothing—absolutely nothing—of the pure unselfishness of their love, are only too glad to take them at their word. Ah, my friend, if you could see your wife's tears when you are gone—tears not all of sorrow for your absence, but tears sometimes of bitter indignation at the contempt you pour upon her by your neglect— then I think you would eat your mutton-chop and drink your glass of sherry on a little table by the sick woman's bedside, and thank God that you had dined well.

After morning school on the day appointed, Mr. Goggs called upon the lawyer.

"Sir," said he, as soon as he found himself in the office, "I have given the two boys a shilling apiece, and I beg to say that I regret, upon mature consideration, having—aw——"

"All right, old fellow," said Mr. Teasel, who had by this time almost forgotten the matter. "Stop and have some luncheon."

The schoolmaster was on the point of explaining, with many thanks, that his presence would shortly be required in his own dining-hall, when the door of the office was burst suddenly open, and two young ladies, each ornamented with a head of bright red hair, raced each other into the room. "Oh, papa!" they both cried at once, far too excited to notice Mr. Goggs,— "oh, papa, what *do* you think? *Have* you heard the news? Some dreadful murderer has broken into Lady Appletree's bedroom and *carried off her baby!*"

CHAPTER X.

LORD APPLETREE SEES A FRIEND AFTER DINNER.

At the close of the festivities held in celebration of little Viscount Russet's christening, the guests assembled to do him honor went their respective ways, excepting only Sir John Montgomery and his daughter, who tarried still at Withycombe. The party, however, was shortly increased by the arrival of the Rev. Ernest Toyle, whom Lord Appletree insisted upon releasing from the bondage of his landlady, until he had recovered sufficient strength to enable him to bear it.

Here the poor curate was weak enough to forget his plain face and his beggary, and to fall hopelessly in love with the beautiful Edith. Think of his impudence! He, an "inferior" clergyman, with one hundred pounds a year, and a sitting-room twelve feet by ten, had dared to imagine himself to belong to the same species on this earth as a Scotchman and a baronet; had dared to believe it not outrageously impossible that he might be found fit to mate with the loveliest woman in Dumplingshire. Think of his impudence, and pity him when his eyes shall be opened to the enormity of his sin!

Very, very soon the opening came. He was not a man to hesitate, when he had once seen his way. He might

be nervous out-of-doors at night, but he knew what
he was about very well in Lady Appletree's drawing-
room.

"Edith, dear Edith! I love you—oh, it's of no
use to try and say how much! Dear, darling Edith!
I can't help loving you, though I am so hideous, and
you are so beautiful; and, though I am as poor as a
rat, and you are tremendously rich—at least, I suppose
so. But look here, Edith. You won't have me, of
course; will you?"

There was no mincing of the matter here. A man
could not well speak his mind more plainly. The two
were playing backgammon in the drawing-room. Mr.
Toyle had escaped thither, after his second glass of
sherry, which was all that was permitted him at present,
and had left the earl and the baronet to drink their
wine together. Lady Appletree was fast asleep in her
snug arm-chair, whence nasal snortings proceeded ever
and again,—echoes from the kitchen-home of early
plebeian days, remembered only now in dreams.

Mr. Toyle was conducting himself in a decidedly
eccentric manner, and Edith had occasion more than
once to call him to order.

"Why, what *can* be the matter with you?" said she.
"That is the third time you have wanted to play one
of my men!"

"I can't help it," he replied. "I am not thinking
a bit about the game." And then he made his declaration of love as above recorded.

"It is your turn," said Edith, who was totally unprepared with her answer. Silly girl! She ought to
have rehearsed the whole scene in her bedroom, and

to have learned every possible reply by heart, the very day she heard that the curate was coming.

"Bother the turns!" said Mr. Toyle, whose love was getting the better of his manners. "Look here, Edith. You have been so jolly good to me. You didn't think, when you and her ladyship were nursing me, and bringing me all sorts of things, that you were making me love you better than all the world. I haven't got a farthing, Edith; but I'll make it up to you, that I will, if you will let me. Of course you could have any one you pleased,—Honorables and Colonels, and Sir Timothys, and all the rest of it. But, suppose you did; why, Edith, they would not treat you well. They would not, really. And what's the good of marrying a swell, if he bullies you, and leaves you all alone? Dearest Edith, I'll do my very best to make you happy—I will—I swear I will!"

"Sh——sh!" said Edith; "I wish I had known you were thinking of this before. It's the most unfortunate thing!"

"Do you mean to say, then," began the curate, "that there is *no* hope for me—no hope at all?"

"Oh, Mr. Toyle! it is not for me to talk about no hope. I am sure I hope with all my heart that you will be happy for the rest of your days. I am very certain that you deserve to be. But didn't you know that I was engaged already to Mr. Pippin? Don't look like that at me, Mr. Toyle. I am so very, very sorry!"

"Engaged to Mr. Pippin! Ah! now I understand. Good-night, Edith. I won't call you anything else— till you're married; and then I shall be dead, or something worse. Tom Pippin! Ah—I like him awfully. I don't know a better fellow than Tom Pippin. But they are all alike with women. So please understand, Edith, that when he throws you over, because he wants to marry the Dowager Duchess of Double Gloucester, poor Ernest Toyle, with his hundred a year, and his ugly mug, and his sitting-room twelve feet by ten, loves you with all his heart and soul, and will give up his whole life to serve you, and comfort you, and shield you from care, and soothe your sorrows in this world, and help you, as best he may, to be happy hereafter in the world above."

The next day the curate invented an excuse for going back to his sitting-room twelve feet by ten, where widow Giles made up for lost time by letting him know the blessedness of being well looked after. It was a pity that she could not write his Sunday's sermon for him, for the poor fellow was scarcely in a condition to write it himself. He could think of nothing but Edith—of Edith, lost to him, and sacri-ficed to Tom Pippin. At last he wrote to his rector, positively refusing to preach, and begging him to edify the devout souls at Withycombe with two of his own ponderous discourses instead of one. Mr. Toyle in his affliction was rather hard upon the devout souls at Withycombe.

It utterly passes my comprehension how the laymen of average intelligence can endure the average sermon. Nine expositions out of ten, as delivered from British pulpits, are—not to be over-critical—a simple waste of time. Why on earth should they be delivered? What is the real worth of this inexorable law which compels the preacher who has got nothing to say to spend five-and-twenty minutes twice every Sunday in saying it? Why should the educated worshiper be perpetually bored by the dreary exhortations of a holy man without an idea in his head, who cannot even write decent grammar? Why should the unlettered and the poor be driven away to the Meeting-house, by the lifeless commonplaces of some fair and ruddy youth, who reads affectedly his grandfather's manuscript in the morning, and his grandmother's in the afternoon? Why should the whole congregation, young and old, be incited habitually to slumber, by the same ancient story, clothed in the same ancient words, and bewailed in the same doleful strain, till every child knows what is coming next, and could stand up and preach it as well as the parson? There can be no shadow of a reason why. The average sermon is a nuisance, and worse than a nuisance,—a wicked device to keep men back from coming to church to pray. And when one thinks what a sermon might be—what, indeed, just once in ten times a sermon actually is—how crowds might be attracted, and hearts be stirred, and souls be won, by a rightful use of the ordinance now so shamefully abused,—one can only pray with fervor, for the sake of clergy and congregation alike, that a remedy may be found. And the remedy is in every layman's hands. The people can make their parson's sermon what they please. So long as they are content to put up with twaddle, so long will twaddle be preached to them. The curate is indeed bound to sit and listen to his rector, and the rector is bound to sit and listen to his curate; because they are both paid so much a year to stay quietly in their places till the service is over. But the laity are paid nothing, and are bound to listen to nobody. Let them simply decline to be worried for half an hour in church by stuff which they would cough down and hiss in the town hall. Let them rise in a body, as soon as they have said their prayers, and walk home to luncheon, leaving the rector and his assistant minister to improve one another's minds. They will find next Sunday that they are better able to sit it out; and that the sermon which used to be scribbled off hurriedly at the very end of the week has been thought over on Monday, and jotted down on Tuesday, and written fairly out on Wednesday, and weeded of its superfluous repetitions on Thursday, and cut in half on Friday, and reduced yet once again to its legitimate duration of twelve or fourteen minutes on Saturday. A man who can't say enough in twelve minutes to set his people thinking for the rest of the week has no business to get up into his pulpit at all.

Very bad taste, is it not, my reverend brother, to speak of sermons in such a way? Yes. And I wonder which is worse—to laugh at bad sermons, or to preach them? to deprecate that "pernicious facility" in sermon writing which is a reproach to our order; or to go on Sunday after Sunday driving men into indifference and infidelity, disgusting those whom you ought to win, abusing one of the very grandest opportunities for good, and wearying the unexampled patience of your hearers, by a performance which you would never dare inflict upon them, unless protected by the privileges of your calling, and the sanctity of the place from whence you lull your little flock to sleep?

The rector preached his two discourses, grumbling very much at his curate's renewed indisposition ; and Miss Rampion presided at the harmonium. It was certainly very hard upon the devout souls of Withycombe.

Miss Rampion was proud of her harmonium. In her eyes, it represented a triumph of ecclesiastical civilization. "When we came here, you know," said that young lady exultingly to a neighboring parson, "there was a horrid oboe, and a couple of dreadful clarionets, and three or four fiddles, and a trumpet, and a drum. But we did away with all that, you know, very soon !"

"Just so," said the parson. "You found the material for an uncommonly good village band, and you set your foot upon it ; putting in its place—what, did you say ?"

"Oh, such a *nice* harmonium."

"A nice harmonium—an instrument which could have been designed for no other purpose than to send half the congregation hurrying out of church in considerable pain. And by way of completing your reform, you abolished Tate and Brady, I presume, and substituted Hymns Ancient and Modern ?"

"Oh, yes, *that* we did. I do so *love* that dear Hymns Ancient and Modern !"

"Ah, most young ladies do. The red edges go for something ; and it is nice to have a collection of Christy Minstrel songs for Sunday, as well as for weekdays. Well, Miss Rampion, I can't say that I congratulate you on your improvements !"

"Why, Mr. Yarrow! I thought you were a good Churchman! and now you are abusing all the nice High Church tunes !"

"Too good a Churchman, Miss Rampion, I trust, to drive out of my church, and mortally offend, half a dozen well-meaning fiddlers, who only wanted a little instruction to become an efficient band. If you had sent the poor fellows over to me, instead of to the Meeting-house, we would have had The May Queen, or Acis and Galatea, in our schoolroom, before the end of the summer. I wish *I* could lay my hands on a couple of dreadful clarionets and a horrid oboe. But you good people, with your High Church reforms, have extinguished music in our country villages for ever and ever."

"Then, pray," asked the rector's daughter, with a sneer, "do you sing Tate and Brady?"

"No, I don't, Miss Rampion. I am not fond of parodies, and I sing the psalms in their proper place, before the first lesson. English literature supplies me with just five-and-twenty hymns which are fit to be sung in church, and the resources of Christian art provide just five-and-twenty suitable tunes. These we shall go on singing, in our humble little choir, till musicians and poets help us to enlarge our number. But I would rather go back to Tate and Brady, and drums and fiddles, and a barrel-organ besides, than desecrate my chancel with negro melodies, or descend to the spoony sentimental familiarities of address with which modern High Churchmen are not ashamed to insult their LORD."

Mr. Toyle paid no more visits to the great house till the baronet and his daughter had gone away, leaving the earl, almost for the first time since his marriage, in the uninterrupted enjoyment of his countess-cook's society. Lord Appletree was a man who all his life long had found his own company more than tolerable. When his house was full of friends, he was very happy; and, when his friends were gone, he was very happy too. Should a snug little party of four or five assist him to dispose of his good things at dinner, he was pleased to give them of his very best; but, should it fall to his lot to dine alone, he was equally pleased to take the very best himself. Such comforts as money could procure consoled in his solitude the Earl of Appletree; and, if his friends could have witnessed the amount of consolation his solitude sustained, they must needs have arrived at the conclusion either that wine in excess is very wholesome, or that his lordship's life would not be prolonged to extreme old age.

One evening early in November, when the earl had dined unusually well; while choice Madeira, which for a wonder had not been kept too long, sparkled in his glass, and claret, on the rug, before the fire, gave promise of yet more glorious delights in the future; while the countess, in her little room up-stairs, nursed the baby, stimulating herself to the grateful duties demanded of her by repeated sippings from a black bottle—"Lady Appletree's secret"—underneath her chair: one evening early in November the butler interrupted Lord Appletree's lonely dissipation by informing him that a Mr. Burdock was in the hall, desiring to see his lordship on most important business.

"Oh, I can't see any one at this time of night," said the earl. "Tell him to come to-morrow."

But Mr. Burdock refused to come to-morrow, and

persisted in urging admittance to-night. "He won't go, my lord," reported the butler.

"He *must* go!" said the earl. "Shut the door."

Mr. Burdock, however, would not go; and the butler, impressed with the sense of half a sovereign just received, came back in the hope of changing his lordship's mind.

"What is his name, Roberts?" asked the earl, relenting.

"Burdock, my lord."

"Never heard of him in my life. What sort of a looking man?"

"Dark, my lord, with an enormous beard. Not quite the gentleman, my lord; but he says his business is of the most tre-*mendous* importance."

"Show him in, Roberts, and come up directly, if I ring. And, look here; just put away the claret till he has gone."

Mr. Burdock was certainly a very dark man, with such a beard as you do not often see. His face was all hair, if we except a low shining forehead, a red nose, and a pair of fierce black eyes. He looked as if he had just escaped for an hour or two out of the woods, and must go back again to sleep. His clothes, by which the butler had probably condemned his pretensions to be a gentleman, were decidedly seedy; and as he advanced into the room the earl became conscious of an odor, steaming from his coat, his whiskers, and his hair, which led to the conclusion that the short pipe he had just left off smoking was an old companion, and lay, rank and stale, in his frowsy pocket. Lord Appletree was too much of a gentleman to show

his disgust, and too much a man of the world to suppose that he had any just cause for doing so. He was
aware that men who smoke are accustomed to proclaim
their taste wherever they go, by carrying short pipes
in their pockets, and wafting an incense of stale tobacco
into every room they enter. What especial virtue the
scent of stale tobacco possesses, that it should be
tolerated more than any other nasty smell, is a solemn
mystery. The man who should venture to perfume
himself and all his belongings with onions, or pepper-
mint, or whatever other elegant odors there be, would
be shunned in any decent society, and be forced to indulge his peculiar weakness in the stable. But the
smoker is king of all the earth. He may saturate himself with his horrible drug, till his books, his curtains,
his coat, his whiskers, and his very breath are an
abomination to every one who comes near him; and,
because it is considered fine to smoke, and muffish not
to smoke, nobody has the courage to tell him that he
is filthy.

There could be no doubt that Mr. Burdock was filthy
—very filthy indeed. Lord Appletree could not remember when so unsavory-looking a creature had ever
been shown into his dining-room before; but nevertheless he begged him to be seated, asked him his business, and offered him a glass of wine.

Mr. Burdock, however, was such a very long time in
coming to his business, that his noble entertainer began
to lose patience with him. "If you really have anything to say to me, sir," he urged at last, "I will
trouble you to say it; for you must be aware——"

"Quite aware, my lord, I assure you," replied Mr.

Burdock, who, after a long deliberation within himself in what character he might best appear, decided that an assumption of extreme impudence was the most likely to serve his turn. "Quite aware, my lord. Under the *peculiar* circumstances"—and here the speaker smiled affably, jerking his thumb in the direction of the staircase—"under the *peculiar* circumstances——"

"I don't know what you mean by circumstances, sir," said the earl, rising from his chair in great anger and opening the door, "but your manner is confoundedly impertinent, and I will thank you to leave the room."

"Wait a moment, my lord," rejoined his visitor, coolly taking up a clean glass, and holding it before the lamp. "Don't think much of that Madeira, my lord; it's corked. So I'll just drink your lordship's and her ladyship's and—and the *little* lord's health in a glass of port, if you will allow me."

"But I won't allow you," cried the earl, ringing the bell furiously. "Get out of the house directly, sir! And, Roberts," he continued, as the butler ran hastily into the room, "if ever you bring a blackguard like that in here to annoy me again, you will leave my service. Take him out directly."

"A blackguard like that—very well, my lord. Perhaps by this day week or sooner you will be glad to hear what the blackguard has got to say. If so, you will find him at the Pippin Arms. Snug little place, the Pippin Arms, my lord. Happy to see you to luncheon, any day you choose to call. Proud to introduce your lordship to a few more blackguards, who will know more about this business by that time than

you will exactly like, if you persist in not going into it
quietly now with me. For Heaven's sake, my lord, be
advised"—and here Mr. Burdock threw off his impudent manner, and thrust his great whiskers, laden with
their horrid fragrance, under his listener's nose, and
whispered, in a voice which would have been tragic
but for the tobacco, a solemn request that the earl
would think better of it, and listen to what he had to
say.

"You may go, Roberts," said the earl at last, when
he had recovered his breath, for the close embrace of
his visitor had fairly knocked him backwards. "You
may go ; but don't go far away, and be ready to come
up the instant that I ring the bell."

"None of your listening at the door, though," suggested Mr. Burdock, with an easy familiarity which
almost made Lord Appletree change his mind. "His
lordship and I shall get on very well without you for
the next half-hour or so ; and, when we want coffee, we
will ring." Then, leaning gracefully back in his chair,
and tapping the points of his fingers together, he began
business.

"You have a nephew, Lord Appletree, I believe?"
The earl signified that such was the case.

"His name is Pippin—*Tom* Pippin, I think?" he
continued.

"Yes, sir, it is," was the reply.

"And he owes a lot of money, a great lot of money,
a most tre-*mendous* lot of money."

"I am sorry to hear it, sir, both for his sake and for
yours, if you are one of his creditors ; but I really do
not see what it has to do with me."

"It has this much to do with you, my lord, that your hopeful nephew has made use of your name—has borrowed thousands and thousands of pounds of one man or another, to be repaid when he comes into this property, every acre of which is entailed ; and now it appears that the property won't come to him at all, but to her ladyship's baby up-stairs. That is what it has to do with you, my lord ; and I am here to-night to find out whether, under the *peculiar* circumstances, you are going to pay your nephew's debts ; and, if not, what amount of personal property you will undertake to leave him at your death, to satisfy his creditors' claims."

"Not one farthing, sir, you may depend upon it ; not one farthing. My nephew's debts are nothing to me, and you, sir, are still less ; so, if this is all the business you have with me, you may retire."

"But it is not all, my lord," returned the other, filling his glass again, while the earl looked helplessly on, fascinated by his cool impudence. "You see, my lord," he continued, "I'm a sort of a money-lender—that's what I am."

"Well, but I don't want any money," said the earl.

"No, my lord," returned Mr. Burdock ; "I don't suppose you do. Noble earls ain't often in want of money. What they want is the pluck to spend it. A hundred thousand a year isn't of much use to a man if his agent only allows him six or seven thousand of it, and tells him that he must employ the rest on the improvement of the property. Well, as I was saying, I'm a sort of a money-lender. I'm not a Jew, though, you understand."

"No, not a Jew," repeated the earl, thinking that his visitor looked extremely little like a Christian.

"But I oblige gentlemen now and then with ready money; and I have been obliging a certain gentleman at Dumplington lately with a goodish deal. Perhaps you don't know my friend Mr. Teasel, my lord?"

"No, I don't," said his lordship. "Your friend Mr. Teasel is not much in my line."

"Ah, I thought not, my lord—he's one of the 'blackguards;' but we professional men, you see, are compelled to mix with all sorts. Well, Mr. Peter Teasel, of the Close, Dumplington, attorney-at-law, has advanced your lordship's nephew from first to last a matter of fifty thousand pounds, of which forty-four thousand four hundred and forty-four pounds fourteen shillings and fourpence farthing have been raised by me. Now, a sum of money like that can be nothing to you, my lord. Be a brick, and shell out, and let Tom Pippin have the pleasure of telling his friends that the coat on his back is paid for. You don't smoke, my lord, do you?" he continued, pulling out of his pocket a lump of Cavendish, and making preparations for cutting it up in slices on a dessert-plate by his side.

"I'll be——"

"Don't swear, my lord; it ain't like a nobleman, you know, and it's very bad for the health besides—especially so soon after dinner. Take a pipe, my lord, and think over it."

"Roberts!" shouted the earl, in too great a passion to remember that there was such a thing as a bell-rope in the room. "Roberts!" but before the butler could

appear, Mr. Burdock had filled and tossed off two
more glasses of sherry, and was moving towards the
door.

"By-by, my lord," said he, affably nodding his
head. "I'll call for the money in the morning.
You'll give it me, all right. It isn't nice to have a
nephew who owes fifty thousand pounds. Burdock is
my name, my lord. Burdock, No. 5 Cat's Alley,
Cornhill. You needn't mind about the butler. I can
find my way. By-by!"

Mr. Burdock, however, could not find his way, for
he turned down the wrong corridor at starting, and
had traveled some twenty yards thereon before he
arrived at an opening. Then he espied, straight in
front of him, a staircase, leading to a gallery; and
looking upwards he espied, as she passed along the gallery, a nursemaid carrying a child. With no clearly-
defined intentions, Mr. Burdock thought he should like
to pass along that gallery too; and thither he proceeded to ascend.

There were no creaking stairs at Withycombe House.
You trod on paths of green and crimson, your foot
sinking half an inch into the velvet pile. The nursemaid had no idea that she was being pursued; and
her pursuer had certainly no idea what he should do
next, supposing he overtook her.

At last she gave him an idea. At the end of the
gallery was an open doorway, leading into a bedroom
lit throughout by the flames of a scorching fire. In a
corner, visible through the doorway, stood a cradle,
sacred to the tranquil slumbers, or the fractious wail-
ings, of John Viscount Russet. Here the infant, who

had fallen asleep in his mother's arms, was somewhat hastily deposited; and here the nursemaid left him, while she ran down to her supper by another flight of stairs.

Bad spirits, hovering around the money-lender's head, whispered to him that he would never get such a glorious chance again. If he could only smuggle the baby out of the house, and make away with it, or hide it, or sell it, or put it out to be farmed, Tom Pippin would have his earldom, and Tom Pippin's creditors would be paid in full. Good spirits hovered near the money-lender, too; for Mr. Burdock was not yet quite given up to villainy; and *they* also had something to say. But the good spirits got the worst of it, as they very commonly do; and Mr. Burdock carried off the child.

The staircase down which the nursemaid had gayly tripped led at once to an outside door, opening on to the gravel drive in front of the house. This door now stood ajar, letting in a streak of moonlight. Mr. Burdock did not trip very gayly down the staircase, for he was a heavy man, and was moreover rather afraid of dropping the child, being encumbered with a greatcoat and an umbrella, which it might have been dangerous to leave behind. But he blessed the open door, and cursed the streak of moonlight, and hurried with his burden down the intricate windings of the shrubbery, devoutly praying that none of the inmates of Withycombe House might be looking out of window.

Bad spirits brought him luck, and guided him safely through the shrubbery, and down the avenue of elms, and past the clump of cedars on the rising ground

above the lake, till he stumbled upon a well-worn pathway leading to a stile. Bad spirits—nay, dear, good,
loving spirits—kept the poor child asleep, and prompted
him to nestle closely into his ravisher's arms. Bad
spirits brought the money-lender to a trout-stream,
over which had been flung a rustic bridge, for the convenience apparently of a cottager whose strip of garden
ran down to the waterside. Bad spirits made him
linger by the edge and watch the ripples dancing on
the silver flood, murmuring delicious melodies to the
silent night, with none but a money-lender to hear.
Bad spirits set him wondering how deep the river was
a little farther down, and whether it soon reached a
mill, and whether the mimic torrent, gushing through
the open sluice some hundred yards away, made noise
enough to drown an infant's cries. Bad spirits said
out boldly, " Chuck the little beggar in !" but their
voice was harsh and horrible, and the money-lender
shuddered at the sound ; and good spirits came and
drove them back into the shades behind, and told them
that they had overdone their work, and lit up the eddies
on the shining stream till a bright young face looked
out, from the pale light lovingly at the tempted man,
and the splashings of the current flowing at his feet·
made music like the laughter of a happy child—a child
who had slumbered in his arms, and clung to him with
soft, unconscious clingings in days long past ; but GOD
had loved him, and taken him to Himself, and spared
him now awhile from his rest in Paradise to come and
save his father from a deadly crime. No, he could not
chuck the little beggar in. He was as his own, and
his own was a baby-saint in the strong keeping of GOD,

pleading now with his baby voice and his baby smile
for the sleeping boy whom he had thought to murder.
Good spirits had the best of it this time; and Mr.
Burdock, of No. 5 Cat's Alley, Cornhill, who had not
said his prayers for twenty years,—Mr. Burdock, the
money-lender, in the face of a sore temptation and a
great opportunity, deliberately chose not to sin, and
for once at least in his maturer life turned his back on
hell.

What, then, should he do? Returning to the house
and giving up the child was penal servitude; and Mr.
Burdock liked to be at large. He would leave it at
the cottage, and declare that he had found it lying in
the lane. The simple country-folk would of course
believe him. He crossed the bridge, therefore, and
passed through the little garden gate and knocked at
the door. The door was opened by that very simple
countryman—Mr. Cuffs, of the Dumplingshire constabulary.

By this time the baby was awake and crying lustily.
Perhaps some wise mamma will say that it could not
possibly have slept so long, and that it ought to have
cried with cold at the first breath of the chill November air. If so, I can only say that it didn't. This
was a particularly good baby, you will please to recollect; and a viscount besides.

"Well, my man, what have you got there?" demanded the policeman, not recognizing in Mr. Burdock's personal appearance much that should command
respect.

Mr. Burdock told his simple story, which the simple
countryman simply disbelieved. "Found it in the

lane, did you? That was a funny thing to do. I've walked these 'ere lanes a good many times, my chap, and I never found a baby yet in any one of 'em."

"Confound your impertinence!" exclaimed the money-lender. "Why, how do you suppose I came by it, then? Take the child directly, and keep it till its mother claims it. I can't stand talking here all night. I've got a train to catch."

"What train was you going to catch, sir?" asked the policeman, rather more civilly.

"10.20 night mail up, at Withycombe Road, if you want to know. Here, take the child."

"Give it here to me," said a pale, careworn woman, who looked very much as if her husband beat her. Mr. Burdock stepped into the room, only too glad to get the baby out of his arms; and Mr. Cuffs shut the door behind him, locked it, seized the poker in one hand and a big stick in the other, and requested his visitor to take a seat.

The money-lender looked eagerly round the room for weapons, but there was no weapon left to him, unless he could handle dexterously a saucepan or a chair. Then he looked at the policeman, and came to the conclusion that it would be a losing game to fight him, even if he should be despoiled of the stick and poker. So he sat down by the fire, and contemplated the situation.

"Why, it's her ladyship's baby!" cried Mrs. Cuffs at last. "I thought it couldn't be nothink else, by all this 'ere lace and satting."

"And pray, sir, how come you to find her ladyship's baby a lying in the lane?" inquired the policeman.

"Now, sir, you had best tell me all about it. I may be able to help you. There ain't no time to waste, neether; for the moment our people at the great house finds it out, they're certain sure to send down to me." And here the policeman telegraphed to his companion, by mysterious winks and smiles, an intimation that members of the force were not above taking a job in hand, if it were made worth their while.

Mr. Burdock knew a villain when he saw one, and justly determined that he saw one now. There was no chance for him but to enter with the man into a partnership of villainy, and forget the voice of his baby by the riverside. He had meant to do right, but good spirits had not made it easy enough for him, and he must set out once more on the road to hell.

"Send the woman away," said he, at length, "and I will tell you all about it."

"Go up-stairs to bed," said the policeman to his wife, much in the tone in which he would have bidden his dog "go home." "And if you was to give the child some suck, maybe he'd shut up his jabber. She had a baby of her own," he explained to Mr. Burdock, "some months ago, and lost it. Now, sir, we'll get to business, if *you* please."

Then was concocted as pretty a piece of rascality as bad men and bad spirits could devise between them. The simple countryman's calculations were simplicity itself. "If I takes this 'ere baby up to the house," he considered, "I shall get a ten-pun note for a doing of my duty, besides the reward of a good conscience, which will be highly gratifying. But if I keeps the infant here, and makes believe that this 'ere chap's a bolted, why, I shall make something tidy out of *him* for a hushing of it up, and very likely be sent off in pursoot by his lordship, with a decentish lot of money for traveling expenses. And what a comfort it 'll be to my dear wife, as has gone through such a deal of suffering, to have a real live young lord to suckle!"

"Well, sir," said he, at the end of a long conversation, "them's my terms. Fifty pounds a quarter paid regular in advance, to whatever address I send. Me and my missus will take the child, and go abroad in chase, and stay there till we catches the perpetrator of this 'ere deed of darkness—or, till the fifty pounds a quarter ceases to come regular. Then we shall return to our native country, after a fruitless search in foreign parts; and if we shouldn't happen to find Mr. Burdock at home when we calls at No. 5 Cat's Alley, Cornhill, perhaps by traveling a little farther westward we may hear of him somewhere else, and light upon the baby, quite by accident, at the same time. If either the infant or his lordship dies, and you gets your cash from Mr. Pippin, the allowance to be doubled so long as we holds our tongues; and if the boy lives till he's eight years old, another hundred a year to be tacked on for the expenses of his education. We'll have all that down in black and white, sir, afore we parts company, and we'll have it signed in your proper name; and so long as you sticks honorable to me, you may depend that I'll stick honorable to you."

"How the devil do you know my proper name?" exclaimed Mr. Burdock, turning pale, and starting from his chair.

"I knows names when I hears 'em, sir, as well as most; and I knows faces when I sees 'em; and I knows false beards from true. You was very prudent not to risk a tussle with me, sir, just now. The beard might have come off, you know, or got itself twisted round behind your neck, like them things the women wears in church a Sundays."

The money-lender ground his teeth with rage at finding himself so completely in the simple country-man's power. But he had to sign the paper, nevertheless; and he did not sign it in the name of Burdock.

" I'm afeard you won't catch the 10.20 up mail, sir," observed Mr. Cuffs, when the transaction was completed; "but perhaps the 11.35 *down* train might take you a trifle nearer home."

" Never you mind whether I go up or down," retorted Mr. Burdock, angrily.

" Would you like to see the baby again before you go, sir, just to say good-by? My missus will bring him down in a minute, if you want to kiss him, or anything."

" The baby be hanged," replied the money-lender, "and your missus too." And then he started off, walking briskly through the moonlight, to catch neither the up train nor the down, but to reach in moderate time a wayside inn, lying in the opposite direction to the station at Withycombe Road; at which inn he had engaged a bed.

The child had been carried off at nine o'clock, but it was half-past ten before his mother missed him, and half-past twelve at least before she could believe that he was really gone. Every corner of the huge mansion was searched, every cupboard ransacked, every curtain drawn. Bells echoed discordant jinglings from room to corridor; maids fluttered in wild confusion from staircase to hall; men shouted and women screamed; the earl raved and swore; and the countess-cook flung herself upon the empty cradle, and felt and felt and felt again, but could not feel the short, chubby legs, and shoulders buried in their fat, or count like treasures one by one the little tiny toes; for all was blank and desolate, and her darling had been snatched away.

At eleven o'clock a servant went off in haste to fetch Mr. Cuffs the policeman, who received instructions to scour the country round, and came back very shortly afterwards to report that he was already on the scent. A person answering to the description given of Mr. Burdock, of No. 5 Cat's Alley, Cornhill, had been observed to hurry through the village, and past the public house on the station road, intent undoubtedly on catching the 10.20 train for Paddington. He bore a suspicious-looking burden in his arms, which might have been a baby, or might have been a pig; but the burden showed no signs of life, and never by squeak or squeal betrayed its interest in the extreme originality of the position in which it was being held. This was conclusive enough. Mr. Burdock had carried the child to London; and the policeman received a commission from the earl to start instantly in pursuit, was furnished with fifty sovereigns for immediate use, and was invested moreover with discretionary powers to exceed that sum by any amount he pleased, if only the infant might be recovered.

" Should you object, my lord," asked Mr. Cuffs, " to my taking my wife along with me? She's an uncommon 'cute woman, though I says it as shouldn't. She'll fish and fish and find out lots of things that a man could never come nowheres nigh. And when we gets hold of his little lordship, as I make no doubt we shall to-morrow, she'll be a bit handier than I should be about carrying of him home."

This proposition seemed reasonable enough, and Mr. Cuffs was complimented on his sagacity. By all means let him take his wife ; and the sooner they were off, the better.

From London Mr. Cuffs telegraphed the information that the perpetrator of the deed of darkness had availed himself of the South Eastern Railway Company's short sea-passage, and had taken two first-class tickets through to Cologne. By the evening's post he wrote at greater length to say that he himself should cross that night, accompanied of course by his faithful wife ; that he had ascertained, for Lady Appletree's consolation, that the perpetrator had a female with him, and that the infant was alive and well ; and further that he would be much beholden to his lordship if he would procure his discharge from the chief constable of the county, so that he might be free to prolong the search into distant parts of the continent, in case the search should have to be prolonged. Should the perpetrator be speedily caught, and his prey be rescued from his grasp, Mr. Cuffs proposed to forego the rural delights of Withycombe, and to seek employment as a detective in some more extended sphere. His wife had displayed such eminent talent for fishing and finding that he could not do her the injustice to bury her any longer in a secluded village so far from town. In any case, therefore, he should be glad to have his discharge; and another fifty pounds or so placed to his credit at some bank in Cologne would enable him to follow the perpetrator's track with greater facility.

Lord Appletree procured the discharge, and sent the fifty pounds; and though he could not but feel, as a county magistrate, that the Dumplingshire constabulary had sustained an almost irreparable loss, he congratulated himself on the happy circumstance that their loss was his gain, and that so able an incipient detective as Mr. Cuffs, and so 'cute a fisher and finder as his amiable wife, could hardly fail to drag the perpetrator of the deed of darkness ignominiously home, and to restore, to his own and his countess-cook's embraces, John Viscount Russet, the Withycombe son and heir.

CHAPTER XI.

MR. GOGGS ACKNOWLEDGES THE RECEIPT OF A VALENTINE.

THE Christmas holidays came and passed away, and the boys of the Dumplington Grammar-School returned to their master and mistress to be farmed for the season.

A very flourishing establishment, just now, had the Rev. Mr. Goggs. The schoolmaster was putting money by. A year's "devotion" to her domestic duties had taught his treasure of a wife what was the very lowest scale of rations on which great hearty growing boys might safely be kept without becoming pale and thin enough to justify the interference of their friends. Pimples, no doubt, would frequently appear, and faces flush unhealthily with exercise which the ill-nurtured frame was not strong enough to bear. But trifling ailments such as these were signs, in the schoolmistress's eyes, of an overfed stomach and a bilious constitution. A couple of days in the sick-room would set all to rights, and so many ounces of meat and pudding might be entered in the housekeeper's book as saved. If a couple of days in the sick-room did not set all to rights, the doctor would be summoned, and

a small commission charged upon his bill. By the
time the pimple had developed into a boil, and the
flushed face had become freckled with feverish spots,
it would be manifest to all beholders that the boy came
of an unhealthy stock, that nothing but Mrs. Goggs's
tender nursing could have kept him alive so long, and
that his parents ought to be made to pay at least ten
pounds per annum extra, in consideration of the un-
wearying attentions he received.   The idea that sickly
faces arose from writing impositions all day long in a
fusty schoolroom, or that pimples were generated by
meager insufficient food, was too preposterous to be
entertained by any one with intellect more acute than
a stupid, prejudiced, grumbling, discontented, ungrateful boy.

In her "devotion" to the boys, Mrs. Goggs grew
more and more assiduous every day.   From opening
hampers, she had now arrived at opening letters—such
was her motherly care.   The postman's bag was laid
on the breakfast-table at eight o'clock, and the letters
turned over carefully one by one with their directions
downwards.   "Please 'em, that's for me!" cried an
innocent child of nine and a half, as he recognized his
father's big blue envelope and great red seal, on his
second morning at school.   The innocent child was
speedily taught to know his place.   His letter was
carried, along with all the rest, into Mrs. Goggs's sitting-room, where notes could be taken of those that
could be readily opened, and conjectures formed re-
specting those that couldn't; and it was delivered to
him after tea, with an intimation that sealed dispatches
were against the rules of the school, implying as they

did a reflection on the schoolmaster's integrity, and that she should very much like to know, should Mrs. Goggs, whether Croft minor's father thought that *she* was going to trouble herself to open his dirty letters to his boy. Croft minor did not fail to request accordingly that his father would conform to the rules of the school ; nor did his father ever thenceforward fail to write to his son regularly once a week, securing his big blue envelope with a seal about the size of two half-crowns, and printing an enormous PRIVATE on the outside. "A very ungentlemanly person, that Colonel Croft, my dear," observed Mrs. Goggs to the farmer. What Colonel Croft's opinion may have been concerning Mrs. Goggs, does not appear.

In Dumplington, at any rate, opinions concerning Mrs. Goggs were for the most part flattering. The motherly woman made friends out of the mammon of gifts which, if welcome to those on whom they were bestowed, could scarcely be considered costly. Attached to the school-house was a large and highly productive garden, the fruits of which were liberally dispensed among the schoolmistress's immediate favorites in the town. Occasionally she had aspired even to extend the limits of her acquaintance by means of some obsequious present of strawberries or pears ; and once at least she had been very handsomely snubbed for her pains. "Nightshade," said she, one morning, "take this fruit with my compliments to Miss Stuart, and mind you don't eat any of it." The boy, blushing with shame, and with tears starting out of his great blue eyes, took the basket, and met Dr. Stuart at the hall door. "My compliments to Mrs. Goggs,"

said the doctor, "and I have not the pleasure of knowing her. If I had, I should suggest that the good
things growing in the schoolmaster's garden were intended not for his friends, but for his hungry boys.
Stay, Willie. I know you won't dare to tell her what
I say, so I'll write it down. Upon my word, I've
half a mind now to take the strawberries, and give
them to *you*, for the fun of seeing you pitch into
them."

"She told me to be sure and not eat any of them,"
said Willie, laughing.

"She didn't! Come, I can't believe that, even of
her. By George, she shall have the message." And
she had it; and she never made insinuating little ad-
vances to Dr. Stuart or his sister again.

Willie Nightshade was one of the very few among
the "founder's boys" who had won their way to
popularity among their schoolfellows at Dumplington.
Tradition had ruled for ages past that the "white
tassel" fellows were snobs; and such traditions are
not lightly broken through. Of Willie, however, nobody thought one atom the worse because his father
made coffins and paid the schoolmaster Nothing a
year. Harry Northcote and Frank Teasel were his
especial friends, but the whole school liked him; and
you might be certain that wherever he went, in boyhood or manhood, he would be liked by all the world.
He was a fine, manly fellow, good at games, plucky in
the miniature perils of schoolboy life, eager after mischievous adventures, and caring no more for old Goggs
than for old Goggs's maternal aunt. But if old Goggs
had had the wit to manage him, Willie would have

cared for him a good deal. There was a tenderness, a gentle winning sweetness, about the boy, which opened many avenues to his heart, for those who knew how to find them. But what had Mr. Goggs to do with tenderness, save in his mutton and his green peas? Half the consideration displayed towards Willie, which he lavished on his asparagus, would have set the boy wondering for days and nights what he could do to show old Goggs that he was grateful. Not many boys can afford to let you see that their affections are strong and their feelings deep, lest you should think them priggish or unreal; but you would never have thought this of Willie. High spirits and exercise had made him a downright English boy; his mother, with early lessons in unselfish thoughtfulness for others, had made him a gentleman; and GOD, working with him in secret hours, had made him something better than either—a child of his very own, pure and brave and true. Willie's home was not a very happy one, for his mother had died when he was only twelve years old, and his father, by way of a set-off against his professional melancholy, had married a fashionable fine lady, covered with affectations, and vulgar to the last degree. She hated children almost as much as Mrs. Goggs; but at least she was honest enough, with such antipathies, not to keep a school.

On Sundays, Willie was a chorister in the Cathedral choir—an honorary office which he was permitted to hold in consideration of his magnificent voice and intense passion for music—honorary, because the estimation in which Cathedral choirs are popularly held forbids that any rank therein should be pronounced

honorable. The associations of a day which had better
be forgotten have taught us that no gentleman can possibly condescend to the position of lay clerk or singing-
man, and that no gentleman's son ought to be asked to
degrade himself by standing up in a surplice and chant-
ing psalms to the praise of GOD. Music, as all the
world knows, is a common, despicable trade. You
enjoy your concert or your pianoforte recital, just as
you enjoy your sweetbread and leg of lamb; but you
would no more sit at table with the musician who has
charmed you, than you would invite your kitchen-maid
to dinner. Without doubt, the musician would sometimes prove queer company. But whose fault is that?
If you will persist in snubbing the entire profession, in
offering not a single prize to those who enter it, and in
forcing men of European reputation to slave for fifty
hours a week at the very drudgery of their calling,
because it does not pay them to cultivate the art artis-
tically, you can scarcely be surprised that educated
men, who don't like being snubbed, should for the
most part seek openings for themselves in a more con-
genial sphere. From the very top to the very bottom,
in every phase of life, musicians are everywhere made
to know that the British public will be good enough to
tolerate them for the pleasure they afford, and will
trouble them to keep their distance when the pleasure
has been afforded. And so it must needs continue to
be, until official appointments in the musical world are
habitually bestowed upon persons of higher rank in the
social scale. The connection between personal caste
and professional duties is closer than many people will
allow; and no man ever thoroughly recovers in the one

capacity a stigma cast upon him in the other. The musician proves queer company at dinner, because you took him from among queer companions, and put him in a false position; because when he was a chorister he made dirt-pies in the gutter, and when he grew up to be an organist you offered him a salary of forty pounds. Let our universities endow their chairs of music with a thousand pounds a year, and our Cathedrals elect none but gentlemen, and sons of gentlemen, into their choirs, and the most foolish of all foolish prejudices will begin to be done away. Then, from the very top to the very bottom, as popular estimation has fixed the order of precedence, will musicians, like other men, be taken for what they are worth. Each one, according to his merits, will hold his own, as he ought to do, with the parson, the doctor, and the lawyer; the profession will become as honorable as it is now not unnaturally despised; the seedy threadbare devotees thereof will retire, and seek a decent competence elsewhere; and we shall no longer feel astonished rather than otherwise when we hear a pianoforte-teacher sound an H, or see him place upon his key-board such a pair of hands as civilized persons commonly display.

The pianoforte-teacher who had the honor of in-structing Willie Nightshade was moderately well at home with all the letters of the alphabet, and was especially proud of his long, tapering fingers and irreproachable hands. But it was little enough that he did for Willie. Progress in music, like progress in everything else at Dumplington, was strictly "optional." If a boy chose to do his work, he did it; if he didn't choose, nobody made him. "Just play

your piece over," the master would say, as he left the
room at the beginning of the lesson ; "I shall be back
again directly."—"Ah, yes," he would resume, saun-
tering in at the end of the half-hour ; "that will do
for to-day. And, by-the-by, Nightshade, you need
not come again this week. I will *give you a holiday !*"
It is thus that masters earn their money in grammar-
schools and academies ; where, as everybody knows, so
much more "individual attention" is given to boys
than at great overgrown places like Eton, or Winchester,
or Harrow.

Willie was a cleverish lad, and one from whose suc-
cesses Mr. Goggs hoped to gain some credit, if his
father should hereafter send him up to Oxford—for
Dumplingshire was a southwestern county, where
Oxford glories were triumphant, and schoolboys reckoned Cambridge as somewhere about on a level with
St. Bees. Possibly the red hood may have dazzled
with its splendor certain youths of an æsthetic turn ;
and it must be confessed that there was nothing specially attractive to the eye in the very dirty-white
garment which hung like a clothes-bag behind the back
of the Rev. Goggs, M.A., when he read Prayers in
chapel. Of course the schoolmaster was far too judicious to let Willie know that his talents were above
the average. Lest the boy should grow conceited over
his gifts, he gave him constantly to understand that he
was a born fool. Six times in every lesson at least
was the well-known anathema thundered out against
the whole form : "Well, I *must* say, that of all the
stupid idiots that *ever* I had to do with since *first* I
kept a school, *you* boys are the stupidest. Your idle-

ness, *and* carelessness, *and* stubbornness are intolerable. I never *did* see such a set of blockheads in *all* my life, I *do* declare." So touching a remonstrance ought, one would think, to have moved even schoolboys to compunction, and brought into their brazen cheeks the consciousness of shame. The fact that the reverend gentleman had said precisely the same thing in precisely the same words to every boy who had ever been up before him with a lesson, may perhaps suggest a reason why the touching remonstrance moved nobody, and produced no impression of any kind.

Willie Nightshade had a facility in the knack of rhyming, wherewith he beguiled many a tedious half-hour in school. Once he ventured to show up an ode of Horace translated into verse, but his judicious master very properly snubbed him, and made him write it out six times in prose. Mr. Goggs never missed a chance of setting impositions. He dealt out thousands of lines with a profusion which proved the uncalculating largeness of his mind. If the lines had been intended to be learned by heart instead of written, and Mr. Goggs had been kept in school to hear them, his liberality in dispensing them might have been less excessive. As it happened, impositions cost him nothing but the trouble of tearing them up when they were done. "I cannot think, my dear," said the Dumplington boy's papa to the Dumplington boy's mamma, as he endeavored, not always with success, to decipher his son's manuscript over the breakfast-table, —"I cannot think what makes Charlie send home such villainous letters! He used to write capitally before he went to school. I am afraid Mr. Goggs does not

practice him much in writing." If the Dumplington
boy's papa could have watched the Dumplington boy
on a fine half-holiday, as he appeared in the schoolroom
with his head upon his desk, scribbling for his life with
a spluttering steel pen at the rate of sixty words a
minute, so as to get his five hundred lines finished by
tea-time, he must have acknowledged that he had done
the worthy man an injustice; that Mr. Goggs gave his
pupils practice enough, and something over; and that
the "excellent schoolmaster" was taking every possible
precaution to insure, not only that the boy should write
illegibly for the rest of his life, but that he should
abstain from injuring his health by too much exercise in
the open air, and should acquire, by dint of incessant
stoopings and contractions of the chest, as pretty a
pair of round shoulders as if he had been, by nature
deformed.

"Let's send old Goggs a valentine," said Willie
Nightshade, on the morning of the 13th of February.
"You can get some awfully hideous ones for twopence,
and that's just about what he's worth. Mother Goggs
is dead certain to send me up in town at twelve, because she knows that I want to jump; and then I'll
buy one."

Sure enough, when school was over, the mistress's
pleasant face appeared at the door, and her pleasant
voice summoned Willie into the passage to receive his
orders.

"Four yards and a half of second-hand flannel,"
reported Willie, on his return. "That's a nice sort of
thing for a fellow to buy! And I am to match this
dirty stuff exactly. I believe it's a bit of one of her

old petticoats ! If Scraggs won't let me have it cheap,
I've got to go to Snooks ; and if Snooks doesn't take
off twopence-halfpenny in the shilling, I'm to tell him
that Mother Goggs won't deal there any more. What
a mean, stingy beggar it is ! Well, anyhow, Goggs
shall have his valentine. I wonder whether I could
get one second-hand for a penny three-farthings !"

The valentine was no great work of art, representing
simply a bottle-nosed gentleman in pink and blue,
with a birch in one hand and a dictionary in the other.
But it answered the purpose sufficiently well ; and
Willie embellished it overleaf with some appropriate
verses, composed expressly for the occasion during his
numerous leisure moments in school. In the evening
it was sent by post ; and in the morning it came safely
to hand,—safely, but not quite punctually, the letters
being, as usual, half an hour late on that day.

Directly after breakfast Willie was sent up in town
again, to bargain for a dozen yards of tape, wherewith
to "bind" the second-hand flannel. On his way he
met the postman, at the sight of whom the boy ran off
speedily to execute his commission, so that he might
get back to school again in time to see the fun. But
Scraggs and Snooks were hard-hearted that morning,
having risen earlier than usual to get their windows
dressed out for market-day ; and they would by no
means consent to Mrs. Goggs's liberal terms. " We
don't do business in that way," said Snooks. " The
lady had better shop elsewhere," suggested Scraggs ;
" for it doesn't pay a respectable house to have dealings
with her."—" Pray, sir, may I ask," added Scraggs's
facetious partner, " does Mrs. Goggs dine you young

gents off second-hand mutton?" Poor Willie, thoroughly ashamed of his errand, tried another street, and shopped elsewhere; but it was nine o'clock before he had succeeded in driving such a bargain as his mistress would be likely to approve.

At twenty minutes to nine, Mr. Goggs rushed into the schoolroom with his valentine, pale as a ghost, and trembling so visibly in his rage that the bottle-nosed gentleman danced about merrily, and the appropriate verses overleaf rustled and fluttered in his hand. And these were the appropriate verses:—

A RIDDLE.

Oh, what a very happy life
   We all might live together,
Through cloud or sunshine, peace or strife,
   And calm or stormy weather,
If only we were rid of one
Who haunts us like a Christmas dun;
Whose name—oh, let it whispered be—
Begins with H, and ends with G.

He acts so plausible a part,
   You ne'er can tell for certain
What mischief lurks within his heart,
   Behind its silky curtain.
No honest purpose can you trace
In his composed and smiling face,
Whose name—oh, let it whispered be—
Begins with H, and ends with G.

He tries to make the true and good
   Distrustful of each other;
He would persuade you, if he could,
   To doubt your very brother.

He is in truth the deadliest foe
That loving hearts can ever know,
Whose name—oh, let it whispered be—
Begins with H, and ends with G.

Then here's a health to friends sincere—
  The friend of upright dealing,
Whose eye is bright, whose conscience clear,
  Who scorns all base concealing!
And ever overwhelmed with shame
Be he who bears that odious name,
Which—scarcely whispered shall it be—
Begins with H, and ends with G.

" Which of you boys sent this thing to me ?" stammered out the schoolmaster. " I must have his name instantly. Who was it, now? If I don't find him out, I'll expel him !"

" Oh, it was *you*, was it ?" he exclaimed, addressing Harry Northcote, who, in spite of the awfulness of the situation, had burst out laughing. " What did you mean by it, eh—eh—eh—EH—EH ?"

" Please, sir, it wasn't me !" said Harry, as soon as the blows showered upon his face and head by the schoolmaster's clammy palm would give him time to speak.

" Then who was it, sir ?" demanded his relative, catching him by the hair. " None of your shuffling, sir; none of your lies ! Do you know who it was ?"

" Yes, sir," answered the boy, indignantly. " I believe I do."

" You believe you do ! Then I believe you had better tell me, unless you want to be publicly flogged, and then expelled."

Harry was certainly an aggravating boy. He did

not treat his distant cousin well.   He might have kept his secret, and refused to betray his friend, without looking up at his master in defiance, and shaking his head, and laughing in his very face.   So at least his master seemed to think ; for he seized him by the collar, and dragged him to his throne at the end of the school-room, and fumbled in the pocket of his copper-colored trousers for a bunch of keys, and unlocked his desk, and snatched up a cane, and commanded the culprit to "stand round."

"What do you mean, sir," he shouted, "by calling me a Hog? eh, sir—what do you mean?"

"Please, sir, I didn't call you a Hog," said Harry, who was grave enough and pale enough now, poor boy, and stood anxiously watching for the descent of the cane.

"Well, then—a Herring," said the schoolmaster.

"Please, sir, it wasn't a Herring either," answered Harry.

"Then what was it, sir?   Come, I see you know all about it.   What other word is there, that begins with H and ends with G? eh, sir, eh—EH—EH?"

"Please, sir, I think it was meant for Humbug," said the boy, who could not help being impudent, though he knew for certain that he was going to be half killed.

Then Mr. Goggs proceeded to half kill him, while Crawford and one or two of the bigger fellows held consultation together on the question whether or not Harry should be rescued, and the schoolmaster unde-ceived.   At last, however, they decided that it would be the truest kindness to all those concerned, even at

the cost of sacrificing the innocent, to leave the reverend gentleman in his error, and to give him un-
grudgingly whatever rope he wanted, that he might
hang himself once for all. And most effectually was
the reverend gentleman straightway suspended. He
had just laid on his fortieth cut, and smashed his fourth
cane, when Willie, along with half a dozen day boys,
ran into the room.

"Please, sir," he cried, grasping the position of
events, "please, sir, it was not Northcote—it was
me."

"Oh, it was *you*, was it?" returned the schoolmaster,
attempting the satirical, with no remarkable success.
"It was *you*. Well, sir, I won't settle with you just
now. It was *you*, was it? Very good. Perhaps you
will oblige me by coming this way. I am to be called
a Humbug, and a Herring, and a Hog, by such as *you*
—the son of an undertaker, and a founder's boy! Very
good. Please to come this way."

So Willie was marched off to a lumber-room at the
top of the house—a species of up-stairs dungeon, lit by
a tiny window eight feet above the ground, where he
had neither chair nor stool to sit upon, and scarcely
room enough to curl his body round upon the floor.
Here the son of an undertaker spent the day, with not
so much as a lesson-book to entertain him, and with
one scanty meal of bread and water for the refreshment
of his mortal frame. Here the founder's boy passed
the night, without a rug to cover him as he shivered in
the cold; forced to crouch down for rest because he
was too stiff to stand, though the draught under the
door, as he leaned against it, cut him through and

through. It was a dearish price to pay for the fun of sending old Goggs a twopenny valentine with appropriate verses overleaf.

Towards morning he dozed off to sleep, and awoke soon afterwards with a strange sensation in his head, as if a shower of gravel had fallen on him, and some heavy substance were tapping at his face. Opening his eyes, and realizing events one by one, he perceived that a Colenso's Algebra, tied to the end of a good, thick rope, had been thrown through the window from the outside, and was hanging down against the wall. Catching hold of it, he felt that he was being hoisted up; but, on reaching the window, he saw that it would be impossible to get through it until the broken glass had been cleared away. This was a long and weary process, as he could only work with one hand at a time; but at last, after cutting his fingers considerably, and tearing his cuffs and sleeves to pieces, by using them as chisels and hammers, he contrived to set the narrow opening sufficiently free from glass to admit of his body being conveniently squeezed through. In less than five minutes afterwards he had stepped out upon the roof, secured a footing on the low parapet which ran along its eaves, let himself down some twelve or fourteen feet by means of a water-pipe in a corner between two walls, and begun with furious appetite to devour some food which his friend Harry Northcote had brought him.

"What a brick you are, Harry!" said he, with his mouth full of mutton pie. "It is so awfully jolly to get out again. I feel as if I had been in prison for a month. How ever did you manage it?"

"Why, you know," said Harry, "that beast Goggs made a speech about you yesterday afternoon, and swore at you like mad for all your wickedness, and gave notice that he should make an example of you this morning at twelve o'clock by flogging you before the whole school and then publicly expelling you. I wasn't going to stand that, you know, so I cut up in town and got some rope and a lot of grub, crawled out on to the leads from one of the attic windows as soon as it was light enough, smashed your window, shoved in the rope, let myself down by the pipe, and —here we are! Hooray!"

"Flog me and expel me!" repeated Willie, putting on the cap which his friend had been thoughtful enough to bring with him. "That's awkward. What on earth shall I do?"

"Do? why, cut home to breakfast, and persuade your dad to take you away. You'll get out of it then beautifully."

Willie shook his head. "Very much obliged, old fellow," said he; "and that reminds me that I have not thanked you yet for the licking you took for me yesterday morning. I was so awfully savage when I saw that brute letting out at you. You really ought to have told him that I sent it. But I won't go home to breakfast, all the same. I'd sooner go back to my prison again, and be thrashed and expelled."

"Ah, I forgot," said Harry, taking his friend's hand, and signifying, with genuine schoolboy delicacy, that he recollected his home troubles. "Then there is only one thing to be done. Stop here you simply sha'n't. Let's walk quietly off to Aleworth. It's

only ten miles. My governor is sure to back us up;
and, if he drives us in again this afternoon, and has a
jaw with old Goggs, the beast won't dare to touch
either you or me."

Willie was still hesitating, when all hesitation came
of necessity to an end, on the sudden appearance of
an individual with whom the Dumplington boys had
long ago declared eternal war. The trustees of Woodruff's Charity had secured the services not only of an
"excellent schoolmaster," and a mistress who "devoted herself to the boys," but also of a strict and
conscientious beadle-in-plain-clothes, who prowled
about the playground as a spy over the young gentlemen's games; so that at all times, in school and out of
school, a wholesome discipline might be maintained.
The beadle was as worthy of the schoolmaster, as the
schoolmaster was worthy of his "devoted" wife.
Whatever opportunity lay within his power, of interfering with such few pleasures as the boys were permitted
to enjoy, that opportunity did Mr. Toadflax eagerly
seize. If a cricket-ball were hit off the green, so that
it rolled a yard or two down the street, the beadle
picked it up, put it in his pocket, and conveyed it
'.ome. If a carriage happened to pass while two little
fellows were running an exciting race, the beadle
interposed his ungainly figure, and stopped the fun—
lest the horses should plunge with terror, or the coach-
man have a fit and fall into the road. Once every
day at least was some incorrigible lad reported to the
master for grossly insulting Mr. Toadflax by calling
him "the most shocking names," or for endangering
his very life by kicking the football "right straight at

him." The name which shocked Mr. Toadflax more perhaps than any other, and that with which the boys took especial delight in honoring him, had been heartlessly and unfeelingly borrowed from the beadle's physical infirmities. Mr. Toadflax waddled. Mr. Toadflax, in his journeyings from spot to spot, employed a method of progression so peculiar as to make some of the smaller boys declare that, if one of his legs was shorter than the other, the other must be shorter still. The countenance of Mr. Toadflax was unwholesome, and his person odious. And Mr. Toadflax was distinguished in the playground by the shocking name of "Game-leg."

Mr. Toadflax was a pious man, turning up the whites of his eyes in church, responding with prominent devoutness, singing hymns with unctuous fervor considerably out of tune, and weeping much at sermons. He professed great reverence for his employers the trustees, and but little for Mr. Goggs or Mr. Teasel, whom he regarded as fellow-servants, on an equality with himself. The trustees encouraged this impression, tending as it did to exalt them above the vulgar herd of parsons, and schoolmasters, and lawyers. And they were right. Persons high in office owe a deep debt of gratitude to the Toadflaxes who humbug them, and cringe to them, and bow down before them, and minister to their importance. If there were no such foils to their dignity, where would their dignity be? To men of ordinary understanding it might probably never have occurred that the trustees of Woodruff's Charity, for the most part professional gentlemen in the town, enjoyed any rank above those other professional gentlemen of whose offices they chanced to hold the patronage. But by the aid of Mr. Toadflax the thing became apparent at once. *He* was a dependent, and *they* were dependents. By associating in their official capacity the clergyman with the beadle, and the beadle with the lawyer, and the lawyer with the assistant beadle who swept up the autumn leaves, it was made plain enough to all beholders that Messrs. Teasel, Toadflax, Goggs, and Duckweed were a set of snobs together, and that the trustees, their masters, stood upon a pinnacle—a pinnacle, shall we say of greatness, or of littleness?—but yet a pinnacle still. And to stand on a pinnacle is pleasant. "They are a narrow-minded lot," said the lawyer to Dr. Stuart, speaking of his patrons. "Narrow-minded!" said the doctor. "You might pack all their minds away in a hat-box, and it would not be inconveniently full."

Mr. Goggs and Mr. Toadflax, however, were excellent friends, being drawn together by the closest bond of sympathy—a common hatred of the boys. Mr. Toadflax liked Mr. Goggs because the master invariably took his part against his young tormentors, and believed all the exaggerated reports which he daily delivered, of their shocking language and their murderous assaults. Mr. Goggs liked Mr. Toadflax, and took his part and believed his lies, because the beadle, in private life a carpenter and joiner, carpentered and joined for Mr. Goggs on easy terms. With a mischievous set of schoolboys hanging about the place, there was always something or other to be mended; and, while Mr. Toadflax was only too pleased to mend for a mere trifle what he knew that one of his mortal

foes had been made to write a thousand lines for breaking, Mr. Goggs was glad enough to receive with favor
the beadle's numerous complaints, in consideration of
getting his odd jobs about the premises executed at a
nominal charge. So it is that in grammar-schools and
academies the pretty little game of battledore goes
merrily on, the boys being the shuttlecocks, and nobody
else being a bit the wiser.

"Hi, there!" shouted Mr. Toadflax, astonished at
the unwonted sight of two boys standing against the
schoolroom wall before seven o'clock on a February
morning. The boys stood against the wall no longer.
Cramming what was left of the food into their pockets,
they bolted across the green, dodged the beadle behind
a lamp-post towards which he had run to cut them off,
and tore away for their lives along the empty streets,
Mr. Toadflax waddling after them.

"I thought old Game-leg couldn't run!" said Harry,
surprised at the beadle's pace. "But he won't catch
us, all the same. We'll take him down into the water
meadows, and give the beggar a ditch or two to
clear."

The water meadows were a great feature in the country round Dumplington, and both Willie and Harry
knew them well. Many a time, when paper-chasing
on a Saturday afternoon, had they taken off their shoes
and socks, and tucked their trousers up above their
knees, and waded through the river at some shallow
spot, or splashed along the irrigated grass, leaving a
track of dimples behind them as they ran. Many a
time, in the attempt to clear a brook, had they slipped
on the wet turf, and tumbled in—sometimes up to their

ankles only—sometimes to their thighs—sometimes even to their very waists, but always scrambling out undaunted on the other side, thinking what a jolly lark it was, and utterly incapable of reflecting that they must either sit in their comfortless clothes till bedtime, or confess to Mother Goggs the full enormity of their sin. If they could only tempt old Game-leg to follow them, this present chase would be better fun than all. And Game-leg was running like a man—running, indeed, rather faster than was pleasant, and positively gaining ground. For Harry was stiff with his forty stripes of yesterday, and Willie was cramped with his day and night in the cold; so that neither of the boys could run their best, and Mr. Toadflax waddled already less than fifty yards behind. The fun was becoming serious, and they must take to the water meadows without delay.

Here the boys shot rapidly ahead, for the beadle could not jump, and was forced to sneak round by the hatches. Once or twice also he mistook the way, and found himself hemmed in between two impassable streams, from the other side of which his young friends stood and laughed at him, recovering their wind as he retraced his halting steps. At last a long dry field, without a ditch to speak of, pumped out of the poor lads what little breath was left to them, and Mr. Toadflax could be distinctly heard panting and groaning in their rear, as he "improved his position at every stride."

"Now for a spurt!" said Harry, who was leading. "I know exactly where we are. There's a lovely jump in the corner by that sluice. Game-leg couldn't do it to save his life, and you and I have been over it heaps of times. Now spurt like mad, old fellow, and we shall sell him!"

It was a lovely jump, indeed. A jump associated with the name of many a Dumplington boy, who had cleared it at such or such a spot, and was renowned accordingly. A jump which boys would walk out a couple of miles to look at and measure on Sunday, and only wish it was Monday, that they might take a good run at it and get well over. A dear little hurdle fence, not three feet high; then a good wide ditch, if you took it at the left-hand corner; or, if you bore towards the right, a mere trifle of width, but some nasty, hard brickwork to be cleared—emphatically to be cleared, because you would break your shins if you fell short of it, and probably break your neck if you came to grief over it altogether. Harry and Willie had leaped it many a time, brickwork and all; but they were tired now, and worse than tired—wet and sloppy and uncertain of their spring. The beadle was scarcely a dozen yards behind, when Harry went at it vigorously, bearing towards the left, cleared the fence, and plunged into the middle of the stream. Ah! Well for poor Willie if he had plunged into the middle too; but he made for the right-hand corner, fearing to fall upon his friend, slipped on the muddy grass, tripped over the hurdles, and pitched literally head first on the brickwork beyond.

"Oh, Willie, Willie!" cried Harry, kneeling down beside him. "I'm afraid it's a case, after all!"

"I've hurt my head a bit," said Willie, in reply, "but I shall be right again directly. Just look at that

fool Game-leg, fondly imagining that he can climb
over the ditch!"

"I tell you what, though," said Harry; "he can
cross by the sluice, if he has the wit to see his way.
Could you get up a minute, Willie, and help me open
the floodgates? Then we may sit here and grin at
him."

"Oh, yes," answered Willie, "I'm well enough."
So the boys opened the floodgates just in time, and
proceeded to chaff their pursuer.

"Come along now," said Harry, after awhile.
"We have stayed here long enough, and we must get
over to Aleworth. By Jove, Willie, your head must
be jolly thick. I never saw a chap get such a crack as
that, and feel it so little."

Then Willie began to talk nonsense—simple, foolish,
unmeaning nonsense—and his friend grew frightened.
For twenty minutes at least he was delirious, and then
he fell back on the turf and spoke no more. In the
extremity of his terror, Harry condescended even to
call out for Mr. Toadflax; but Mr. Toadflax had disappeared. The beadle was sneaking round by a circu-
itous route, and he soon afterwards waddled up to the
spot where the boys were lying.

"Now, young man, I've caught you," said the
beadle, triumphantly seizing Harry by the shoulder.
"You'll just come along with me, and your precious
friend there with you."

"Don't you see that he can't move?" returned the
boy. "He is hurt most awfully, and I am afraid he
will die."

"Die! stuff and nonsense! he is only shamming."

And here the beadle left Harry to himself, and shook the wounded boy roughly by the arm.

"Leave him alone, you cruel brute!" cried Harry, springing upon the man so fiercely that he retreated towards the brook, where one game-leg got entangled in the other, and the beadle fell ignominiously backwards.

"Oh, Master Northcote, help, help, help!" he exclaimed, as he floundered about in the water. "I can't swim, and I shall be drownded! Help, help, help!"

"Swim, you great muff!" said Harry, with contempt. "Why, it's only five feet deep; and as for help, you may get out how you can."

Mr. Toadflax, thus reassured, got out speedily, and made the best of his way home along the road; being subject to rheumatics, and dreading nothing so much at any time as cold water. Besides, he had sense enough to see that poor Willie Nightshade stood in need of better help than he could give him, or Harry either; and his first visit on his arrival at Dumplington, after changing his wet clothes, was paid to the undertaker, who drove off instantly to ascertain the worst about his boy.

Soon after the departure of the beadle Willie revived, and talked more rationally to his friend. But his mind was ever wandering back to school scenes, and he burst again and again into fits of laughter, at the remembrance of tricks which he had played old Goggs.

"My head feels very queer," said the boy, after a long silence. "Do you know, Harry, I believe I am going to die."

"Not you," said Harry, trying to cheer him up. "Don't talk about dying, Willie, for goodness' sake."

. "Ah, but I am, though. It seems hard to die, Harry, just for sending old Goggs a valentine. But, I say, it was awful fun, wasn't it?" And here he laughed unnaturally, and began to ramble.

"I know all about it now," he said, when he came to himself again. "I am really going to die. And, Harry, I want you to promise me something. When I am dead, don't let them put me into a coffin. Please don't. You won't, now, will you?"

"You are not going to die, Willie; and you are talking stuff. Of course we shall all be put into coffins, some day or other."

"But *I* won't. I won't. I *won't*. Oh, Harry, dear, dear Harry! I thought you would do that much for me! I would do anything for you; but I can't do anything, because I am going to die. Please be kind to me. Please do. Oh, if you knew how I hate the sight of a horrid black ugly coffin! Don't let them make one for me!" And the poor boy flung himself on his friend's neck, and burst into tears.

Harry began to comprehend him now. The undertaker's son had seen enough of coffins, and hearses, and plumes; and he wanted to be buried like a Christian. So Harry promised him that, when he was dead, he should be dressed in his surplice, and placed on a simple board, and carried to the grave by his schoolboy friends, and laid in the earth as a boy who should one day rise again, instead of being nailed down in a hideous box by drunken workmen, and pushed away out of sight, as if there were to be an end of him forever.

Soon after this, Willie began to say scraps of lessons, and play football over again in his delirium, stopping short from time to time to laugh at the reverend schoolmaster, or imitate Mother Goggs as she was giving some little chap a jaw. But never word escaped his lips which his mother or sister might not hear. Suddenly he became quiet again, and turned round to Harry, complaining of strange noises in his head, but looking as well as ever. "They are all singing to me, Harry," he said. "Can't you hear? Oh, it sounds so awfully jolly! Ah—that's the anthem I like best of all. Say it to me, Harry. I can't recollect the words."

"I don't know what you mean, Willie—really I don't. Try to go to sleep, that's a dear old fellow."

"What a brute that Goggs is!" observed Willie, rambling again. "He is such a spiteful beast. I don't believe any fellow likes a master a bit the worse for licking him if he deserves it; but everybody hates a chap who is always badgering and bullying, and won't believe a word you say. Mind you don't eat any of them, Harry, if Mother Goggs sends you out with strawberries. Ah—now I can hear the words. 'O remember not the sins and offenses of my youth'—sins and offenses of my youth—such a lot of them, Harry! Oh, I *am* so sorry. GOD forgive a poor, wicked boy! 'But according to thy mercy think Thou on me—think Thou on me—for thy goodness.' Such a lot of them, Harry! I wish I hadn't sent that thing to Goggs. But I say, Harry, what a jolly lark it was!"

"Do you think old Goggs will go to heaven?" asked the boy, after another fit of dozing.

"Oh, yes, I suppose so," replied his friend. "Clergymen always do."

"Well, I hope he will. But do you think he'll go in that old school-coat? I am afraid he hurt you tremendously yesterday morning? What a brick you were not to sneak of me! But I *must* say, that of all the stupid, careless, idle dunces that ever I had to do with, you boys are the stupidest. Write out a thousand lines apiece, and—— Oh, Harry, Harry, hold me up a minute! my head is so awfully bad!"

"Don't try to talk, Willie. Keep yourself quiet. Somebody will be sure to come directly and fetch us home."

"Somebody fetch us home? but I *won't* be fetched. I *won't* be squeezed into a nasty trunk, and hammered down in the middle of the night, as if I were going to be sent off by luggage-train, this side up, with care."

"No, you sha'n't, old fellow; you sha'n't, really. I'll tell your dad about it."

"My dad—ah, how sorry he will be! Give my love to him, Harry. I wish Frank was here. Give my love to him, too; and to Tom Pippin, and dear old Grab. Don't you remember how we used to laugh at boys always dying in books? and now it has come true. Oh, I am so sorry for such a lot of things. GOD forgive a poor, wicked boy! only a boy! Good-by, Harry—— What a row those fellows make! I can hear them singing still. 'O remember not the sins and offenses—of my youth'—say it for me, Harry. I can't think what comes next."

Harry said it, as best he might, for he was half choked with sobbings over his first great and bitter grief. But he said it to himself alone. Willie had been fetched home indeed. He had gone on a longer journey than his friend could ever take him. He was safe in the keeping of One who, though He had often mourned over his schoolboy follies, and sometimes pleaded with his wayward heart in vain, had once for love towards children become a boy Himself, that He might know what the perils and temptations of boyhood were.

CHAPTER XII.

THE MAD ENGLISHMAN TAKES A PLUNGE.

THE two highly sensational reports, that Lady Appletree's baby had been carried off, and that Tom Pippin
was engaged to Lady Maria Bent, burst simultaneously
upon the ancient city of Dumplington. Simultaneously; for indeed they could hardly have burst otherwise. Had the one report exploded before the other,
the other would never have exploded at all. If his
little cousin were smothered or drowned, Tom had no
need to marry the cripple. If Tom married the cripple,
his little cousin had no need to be smothered or
drowned. And, in that the events had happened simultaneously, Tom felt himself to be an ill-used man.
The perpetrator of the deed of darkness, whoever he
was, might surely have either perpetrated it somewhat
earlier in the week, or at least have given Tom just a
slight suspicion of the nature of his designs. Tom
would have scouted as a thing poisonous and horrible
the bare thought of even winking at such a crime; and
yet it would have been convenient upon the whole to
postpone the gushings of his love for Lady Maria, and
to refrain from recalling his sweet reminiscences of her
infancy, until he knew for certain that there was no
possible way of escape from his troubles but the way of

her golden charms. It is more than probable that Mr. Burdock, as he listened to the pattering of busy feet upon the pavement, and heard the swinging to and fro of chop-house doors, from his office stool at No. 5 Cat's Alley, Cornhill, may also, regarding the matter from his point of view, have felt himself to be an ill-used man; inasmuch as Tom Pippin, if he had only been civil enough to revive his impressions of Lady Maria's childhood three days before, would have saved the money-lender from the necessity of cultivating the very undesirable acquaintance of Mr. Cuffs the policeman.

Nevertheless, now that he had done it, Tom was man enough to stick to it. He had no idea of shilly-shallying about, making a fool first of one woman and then of another. He had chosen his line, and it was not such a bad line after all. Everybody told him that he had done the right thing. One fault only had ever been charged upon Tom—the black, deadly sin of poverty; and now, with estates of unknown wealth in all three kingdoms, Tom would stand faultless in the sight of his fellow-men. The duke was delighted, the earl was charmed, the young lady was radiant with gigglings in anticipation of matrimonial bliss. Tom Pippin was at least contented; and who besides had any business to interfere? There was Edith, to be sure; but Tom did not allow himself to think very much about Edith just now, though he could not doubt that she would admit, on calm reflection, the wisdom of his ultimate choice.

Christmas Day arrived; and the amateur detective, aided by his 'cute wife, had been fishing and finding at Lord Appletree's expense for the last five weeks, but had fished and found nothing as yet, except the tantalizing fact that the perpetrator was always just in front of him, that he was always just going to catch him, and that he always just contrived to get away. Captain Northcote, who had his own ideas about Mr. Cuffs, rode over once or twice to Withycombe and imparted them to the earl.

"I can't think," he said, "why you allow yourself to be humbugged by that fellow. He has got your child safe enough; and he'll keep him, so long as you make it worth his while."

"My dear friend," replied the earl, "it isn't a bit of use to talk. I'll never believe a word against Cuffs. Besides, what could possibly be his motive?"

"Ah," said the captain; "there you beat me. The motives of gentlemen like Mr. Cuffs are not so easy to fathom. But look here, Lord Appletree. Will you give me leave to go in search, quite on my own account, and try *my* hand at fishing and finding? I won't compromise you in any way whatever; and by this day week I'll bring the baby back again."

The earl, however, would not hear of it. He placed unlimited confidence in Mr. Cuffs, and almost unlimited funds at Mr. Cuffs's disposal. He shrank with horror from the publicity which Captain Northcote, by some fiery act of vengeance on an imaginary perpetrator, would bring upon his domestic trouble; and he wished to draw down neither the world's pity nor the world's ridicule upon himself or his countess-cook.

On New Year's Day the worst of it was told. A letter came from Mr. Cuffs, saying that the child was dead. He had tracked Mr. Burdock as far as Basle, and the two men had slept almost in adjacent rooms. But the money-lender, before retiring to rest, had "stood on the bridge at midnight," had dropped the infant into the rapid stream, had breakfasted half an hour before the policeman, and vanished — Heaven only knew whither. The deed had been witnessed, and the fact was beyond dispute; and there was nothing left for the countess and the earl but to go mourning for their child.

One thing besides was left—the least little dawning suspicion that Mr. Cuffs was not quite true. Suspicion, in such a matter, was ground for immediate action. The earl and the captain started off together, attended by a couple of detectives from London; followed the policeman step by step till they came to Basle, and then missed him suddenly; gathered intelligence enough of the crime on the bridge at midnight to justify a belief that the baby had actually been thrown into the Rhine; offered rewards for the apprehension of Cuffs, and heard no more about him; and finally returned to England, in the full conviction that the little viscount was a viscount no more.

And so in course of time the happy day was fixed, and drew near, and dawned, which was to unite the handsomest man in Dumplingshire with the ugliest woman in the world. May was the happy month; and the happy scene of the interesting ceremony was the parish church of Crookleigh St. Andrew, where dukes for generations past had pillowed their ducal heads on the cushions of the ducal family pew. It was a truly ducal sight, and the whole county was there to see. The rich old man who married his cook to please

himself had smuggled the lady up to London in the
dark, and wedded her at some dingy, unfrequented
church, in the presence of his flunky, his cook's wait-
ing-woman, and the sexton. The good-looking young
rake, who was going to marry a dwarf to please his
creditors, had scarcely room enough to make his way
to the altar, between the ranks of smiling daughters
and well-born dames who kissed their congratulations
towards him, and showered the customary and highly-
esteemed blessings on his path. A man may not marry
his grandmother, or his cook. The one would be old-
fashioned, and unpleasantly precise ; the other would
clip her H's, and very possibly bite her nails. But a
man may marry an idiot or a dwarf, if only he will
shut the creature up out of society's way, and spend
her money freely on the darlings who ride with him,
and dance with him, and dote upon him because he is
such a dear duck of a fellow, and treats his misbegotten
incubus of a wife so well. Lady Maria need scarcely
have distressed herself with the apprehension that her
marriage with Tom Pippin would bring him into contempt with all the world.

And so the happy day dawned, and shed its early
streaks of light, and blazed in the full splendor of
approaching noon ; and Tom Pippin's best man led
him up to execution in the sight of the enraptured
crowd. The bridegroom's face was deadly pale, and
his brow wore a look of intolerable anxiety, as if the
cares of the estates in all three kingdoms were already
beginning to weigh him down. At every step, as he
advanced towards the spot where his blooming bride
awaited him, did the burden of anticipated wealth seem

harder to bear; and when at last he stood beside her, and the bishop's chaplain began to read his office, poor Tom gazed up into the minister's face with a look of such hopeless misery, that the minister stopped in the middle of his exhortation, and beckoned to the clerk, and bade him open the chancel door to let in the cool spring breezes, and fetch a glass of cold water from the vestry, in case the gentleman should faint away. But the gentleman stood horribly erect, like a corpse in wedding-garments set on end ; waxing paler and paler as the time for joining hands drew near; the very Statue of Desperation, the Monument of The Man who might never hope again. For Tom had dined out the night before in Dumplington, and Edith had sat at table with him; and Tom had taken her hand and pressed it, and tried to excuse to her his villainy; and she had turned from him gently, with her old bright, sunny smile, and muttered with broken voice, in the dear old tones that might, if he would, have welcomed him home forever, a wish that he might be always happy, and an assurance that she herself had nothing to forgive. And Tom had thought only of Edith, and Edith's voice, and Edith's touch, and Edith's smile, and Edith's love which he had lost, from that time to this. All night and all the morning he had cursed himself, slumbering and waking, tossing his head on the pillow from side to side, or pacing his bedroom carpet to and fro ; now forgetting for awhile his wretchedness, and then starting up with a cry of anguish, as he remembered it again : but always cursing himself, and himself alone, for the curses stored up against him by his own stupendous folly. Within a very little was Tom of doing what many a man has done with less excuse, as he felt the edge of his razors one by one, and sat before the looking-glass trying to make up his mind, and wondering whether it hurt, and what would happen afterwards, and how the world would take it, and whereabouts it was best to begin.

He was wishing he had done it, and swearing to himself that he would not miss another chance, when the Bishop of Dumplington stepped forward from the ecclesiastical easy-chair in which the Vicar of Crookleigh St. Andrew had decently enthroned him, and demanded of the bridegroom the customary declaration.

" Wilt thou have this woman to thy wedded wife ?" began the bishop, reading the paragraph with wonted episcopal impressiveness to the end. But Tom Pippin made no answer, and gave no sign.

The bishop thought Tom a very extraordinary young man, and signified to his chaplain a desire that the bridegroom should be prompted to the performance of the duties required of him. The chaplain whispered to Tom, and Tom stared vacantly at the chaplain, but his lips never so much as moved. The chaplain fetched his book, and pointed to the response which Tom was expected to make, but all in vain. At last the bishop, with some little asperity of manner, read the question over again, coming close to the interesting couple as they stood together, and impatiently awaiting a reply.

"Don't you understand?" asked his lordship, angrily, thinking that Tom was making a fool of him. "You have got to answer, you know."

"Aw," said Tom, at last; "aw—beg your pardon,

but—aw—didn't quite catch—aw—would you mind aw saying it again?"

The bishop, who had a great regard for dukes in general, and the Duke of Dumplingshire in particular, vouchsafed to read his question for the third time; but Tom had no answer ready. "The man must be mad," thought the bishop, retiring in great wrath to his ecclesiastical easy-chair.

"You had better try him once more," whispered his lordship to the chaplain, "and tell him that, if he does not speak next time, I shall stop the service. I have no notion of being played with like this."

"Wilt thou have this woman to thy wedded wife?" began the chaplain. "Now, mind," he continued, in a lower tone; "when I come to the end, you must say, 'I will.' Do you understand?"

"Aw—I was just aw thinking whether I would," muttered Tom. "By Jove, you know, she's so short, you know, and aw—would you mind aw saying it again?" And here, for the first time since he had entered the church, the bridegroom turned half round and looked into the face of his blushing bride. She herself had evinced no sort of interest in the momentous question three times repeated by the bishop, or shown surprise at Tom's eccentric method of dealing with it. Her features wore their habitual grin of idiotcy, as she rocked her comely person from side to side; and the bishop watching her movements wondered within himself, if Tom were so troublesome to manage, what on earth he should do to preserve his dignity before the congregation when he came to Lady Maria. Now for the first time Tom looked into her face, and

then recollected all about another face; and then it
was all over with Tom.

"Wilt thou have this woman to thy wedded wife?"
asked the chaplain, yet once again.

"No, I'm *blest* if I will!" said Tom, unmindful
alike of the sanctity of the place, the high office of
the bishop, and the solemnity of the occasion. "You
see, old fellow, it's aw impossible. She is so awfully—
aw"——And here, the cool spring breezes as they rustled
through the chancel door suggesting a way of escape,
Tom picked up his hat from the pavement, bolted into
the churchyard, ran for his life to the village public-
house, in front of which a groom was leading a horse
up and down, seized the bridle from the servant's
hand, sprang on the creature's back, and rode at full
gallop to the station at Dumplington, where he arrived,
by a wonderful piece of luck, just in time to catch the
London train.

Such a scene the walls of church or chapel had never
witnessed yet, since church or chapel first began to be.
Some slight sensation of smothered merriment had
been apparent among the dowagers and darlings in the
nave when Tom first refused to speak; but his hesitation was for the most part assigned to nervousness, and
nobody supposed for one moment that he meant to
shirk his engagements. But when they beheld him
darting through the chancel door the entire congregation appeared to forget, almost as effectually as Tom
had forgotten, that they stood on holy ground.

"Stop him!" cried the earl, calling out to a group
of servants who were looking on from the belfry tower.
"Stop him! he's as mad as a hatter!"

"Mad!" muttered the duke, hurrying out of his pew. "If I catch the vagabond, I'll drag him back and horsewhip him!"

"Oh—oh—oh!" shrieked the dowagers.

"Ew—ew—ew!" simpered the darlings.

"By Jove—aw—what a vewy odd fell-aw!" said a chorus of British aristocrats, screwing glasses into their eyes.

"Gentleman changed his mind, it seems," said one flunky to another flunky, grinning under the belfry tower.

"Sh——sh!" said the bishop, whose presence of mind had fairly deserted him at the first shock of Tom's unprecedented flight. "Sh——sh! Remember, good people, that you are in church. Kneel down in your respective places, that I may give you my blessing."

The good people did not kneel, because kneeling is vulgar, and *they* were nobly born, or, if not nobly born, were distantly connected with those who were nobly born, or, if not in any way connected, had shaken hands or dined with those who were nobly born, or, if they had never dined, had dined at least with the friends of persons who had shaken hands with those who were nobly born. So they did not kneel, but they expanded their draperies into small balloons, and squatted, in a position not only extremely elegant but indicative both of gentle birth and good breeding. If they could but have been photographed as they appeared while undergoing the episcopal benediction, and their likenesses could have been transferred to the pages of the *Illustrated London News*, all England would have wondered, first, how the poor creatures got themselves into such a remarkable attitude, and secondly, how they ever contrived to get themselves out of it.

So the good people were dismissed, and hastened into the churchyard, where they wandered unquietly among the tombs, standing, unmindful of the dead, on grassy mounds, or climbing on to slabs of granite, in the hope that they might catch a glimpse or two in the distance of the knight who had loved and ridden away. Half a dozen men on horseback started in pursuit, charged by the duke to bring the knight back to his castle, alive or dead. But the knight was too many for them. The village clock proclaimed the canonical hour of twelve. The dowagers sailed into their carriages ; the darlings grouped themselves grace-fully in their seats ; the British aristocrat ordered out his drag ; the bishop resigned the ecclesiastical easy-chair and walked into the parson's study to disrobe ; the bridegroom's best man looked supremely foolish and made believe to recover his self-possession by lighting a cigar ; and the bridesmaids bustled their queen into the vestry and locked the door, in antici-pation of the inevitable fainting-fit, which, contrary to all established precedents, stubbornly declined to ensue.

"Bless your souls, my dears, I'm all right," said Lady Maria. "Don't you alarm yourselves, by any means. I knew it would never come off. There, don't you go untying my strings! Let's get along home. I want some luncheon. Oh, no, I forgot. It's *breakfast* that people have for an early dinner the day they are married. Lady Betty Blackthorn, I'll

just trouble you to leave my hooks and eyes alone.
If I am a dwarf, that's no reason why I should be
undressed before company!"

"Well, but, dear," said a chorus of sweet creatures, "consider the situation,—how very distressing
it is!"

"Distressing! not a bit of it! I knew very well I
was too ugly for him. Oh, Tom, Tom! why didn't
you come and marry me in my infancy?"

Between the intervals of his varied benedictions on
the bridegroom, the Duke of Dumplingshire was hospitably endeavoring to persuade his wedding guests to
stay and eat his daughter's wedding breakfast, wedding
or no. Of course it was out of the question that any
such invitations should be accepted. "Bishop," said
the duke, as the episcopal carriage came round, "you'll
take a bit of luncheon before you go?"

"No, thank you, duke," replied the bishop, highly
indignant at being trotted out for nothing. "Straight
home," said his lordship to the footman; and, as the
episcopal horses whirled him away, he muttered to
himself yet other little words, which neither footman
nor duke might hear.

The Great Western Express brought Tom to Paddington at six o'clock, and a cab soon afterwards set
him down at the door of his uncle's bachelor establishment in Bolton Street, May-Fair. Here he dined off
a hastily-prepared beefsteak, not caring to encounter
the publicity of his club; and, having filled a small
portmanteau with clothes and other necessaries, of
which he was accustomed to keep a supply in town, he
caught the evening train from London Bridge, crossed

the Channel at midnight, and breakfasted at Brussels in the morning. " There is only one chance for me," said Tom to himself, as he counted out his money at the hotel. "I must cut away to Switzerland, and walk it off. Here's ten, fifteen, twenty, twenty-five Napoleons. By Jove, that won't go far." It was all, however, that Tom could reckon up. The duke had taken a check with him to church, to be sensationally pressed into his son-in-law's hand when the wedding was over. But his son-in-law would not wait to earn his money. Tom still owed fifty thousand pounds; and now, with his matrimonial projects abandoned, unless he could sell Ribstone Court, he had no means of raising fifty thousand farthings.

Tom had never been to Switzerland before. He could not tear himself away from the attractions of an English summer. Cricket, rowing, archery, fishing— these were his amusements, and they had always kept him at home. He was glad, therefore, to glean a hint or two, at the table-d'hôte, from an American gentleman who appeared to have "done" everything in all the corners of the earth, and something to spare.

From this most entertaining individual Tom learned that it was now full early for Alpine work, and that he had better take the Rhine leisurely on his way. Tom started, therefore, on the morrow for Cologne, whence he made his way quietly down to Heidelberg and Baden-Baden ; where, with his usual luck, he staked a few Napoleons for fun, and won upwards of a hundred pounds.

This was on the 1st of June ; and Tom, overjoyed at his accession of wealth, went down to Lucerne, and "did" what everybody else has done, until he knew the *diligence* roads and horse-paths of the Oberland moderately well. Then he fell in with a party of friends from England, who laughed at him for lingering in scenery so " tame," and carried him off to Zermatt, where they promised to show him, on the snow-fields of Monte Rosa and the Matterhorn, what Switzerland really was. These gentlemen rejoiced in ice-axes instead of alpenstocks ; prided themselves on a decided preference for populous beds and nasty food ; thought it fine on all occasions to pretend that they liked to "rough it ;" and wrote long-winded accounts of their mild adventures in the visitors' book, making many mistakes in spelling, and adding to their signatures the coveted symbol A. C.

"Rough it !" said Tom, when his friends chaffed him at the inn on the Riffel for grumbling at a mutton-cutlet of which no sheep on this earth could ever have been guilty ; "rough it ! it is not a question of roughing it ! We have not discovered a country, or been shipwrecked among a set of savages. If we had, I would back myself to 'rough it' as good-humoredly as the best of you. This is a place where hundreds of Englishmen spend hundreds of pounds every year. Why in the name of common sense should a man be forced to eat filth, and lie awake all night, when he is working like a horse, and wants better food and sounder sleep than usual? It's all affectation and humbug. There is no particular merit in choosing to put up with dirt, when you might easily be served with what is wholesome and clean ; and, as for the supposed *manliness* of the idea, it just happens to be an invention of

the women. Your young-lady-tourist won't believe
that she has been out of England if she does not go
home poisoned and bitten to death; and these rascally
innkeepers, knowing her weakness, have the wit to take
good care that it is thoroughly well gratified."

The perilous exploits which his friends recounted at
dinner, or recorded in the hotel-books, entertained
Tom Pippin exceedingly. It appeared that, with the
assistance of Christian Anderegg, Franz Taugwald,
Ulrich Almer, Jacob Michel, and seven or eight por-
ters, these adventurous Englishmen, three in number,
had been over all the passes in the district, and climbed
every peak of any consequence, from the Weisshorn
downwards. Think of their bravery! And they were
not only brave, but scientific also. Wherever they
went they took observations, and left thermometers,
describing in the aforesaid visitors' book the spot on
which the instrument would be found. Tom was much
impressed with their deeds of daring, and requested to
be informed whether it were possible for a humble individual like himself ever to become a member of the
A. C.

"You must go up a certain height, you know," said
one of his friends, "and do three or four swell things
out here; and then we could put down your name."

"But I must do the swell things *by myself*, I suppose?" rejoined Tom. "I must not have a lot of
guides to help me?"

"Oh, yes, you may—as many as you like. Only it
comes rather expensive, you see, when you have more
than three to each man."

"Then I don't think much of your exploits," said

Tom. "If a fellow, or two fellows, or, if you please, for safety's sake, half a dozen fellows tied together, can get over a glacier, and up to the top of a snow mountain, all honor to the chap that gets up the freshest. But if they are to have a couple of natives apiece to show them the way, and cut steps for them in the ice, and haul them up with ropes, then for the life of me I can't see what they have done to make such a mortal fuss about." And Tom, wishing to be in the fashion, and anxious to contribute something towards the embellishment of the visitors' book at Macugnaga, inscribed therein the following lines :—

A gallant young "Alpine" ascended a slope,
His body bound round with a furlong of rope ;
    And guides half a score
    Behind and before :
" Hurrah !" he exclaimed ; "why, *I've done* the Weiss Thor !"

His small brother Fred, when he heard of the feat,
Scrambled up through his window, tied on to a sheet.
    " Oh," cried he, " mamma dear !
    Do just come and look here !
I can *climb up a wall*—I'm a Swiss mountaineer !"

The moral comes home, gallant "Alpine," to you :
If you must brag at all, brag of *what you can do*.
    O'er these heights so appalling,
    Any child might go crawling,
With guides by the dozen to save him from falling.

At Macugnaga, Tom parted company with his enterprising friends, and went down to Baveno, to get a decent dinner. A catastrophe had just come to pass at Baveno. A gentleman, living at a pension close by, had hired a boat that afternoon, and gone for a row on the lake. The water looked very tempting, and the gentleman thought he should like to bathe. He pulled off his coat and waistcoat; and the Italian, who was wielding two enormous oars at the extreme end of the bows, stopped rowing, and stared. The gentleman smiled at his look of consternation; took off the rest of his garments one by one; rolled them up in a bundle under the seat, that he might protect, as far as possible, his watch and purse; stood, destitute of clothing, on the gunwale of the boat; and swung his arms round and round, while he made up his mind about plunging in. At each step in the process of unrobing, the youth in the bows had manifested ever-increasing signs of terror. So wild a supposition never entered into his head, that any man in his rightful senses could undress in a boat, and shamelessly expose his naked body to the blushing gaze of an Italian sky. As for *bathing*, the lad had never heard of the lake being applied to such a purpose in his life; and, if he had, he would not have believed it possible that any one short of a maniac would choose to bathe in water a thousand feet deep, when he might paddle up to his waist on the muddy bank in comparative safety. No, it was all plain enough. The man had hired his boat with the deliberate intention of committing suicide; and he, the unoffending boatman, would have to answer to the authorities for connivance at the crime. With a scream of horror he sprang forward from his seat, just in time to see the Englishman, whose balance had been effectually upset by the Italian's movements, fall—certainly not head first—into the clear blue water.

The Englishman was a moderately strong swimmer,

and, being cheated out of his header, determined to enjoy in its stead the luxury of a good long dive. The Italian watched and watched, but the body of the wretched maniac did not come up again. Alas! it never would come up again! and *he*—what *should* he do? At any rate, he would act the part of innocence, and lose no time in raising the alarm. He seized his oars, therefore, and rowed hastily back in the direction of the nearest island; where he gave information that a mad Englishman from Baveno had hired his boat, had stripped himself to the skin before his very eyes, had flung his body into the lake, and had sunk to the bottom like a stone.

When the mad Englishman rose to the surface from his dive, he swam a couple of hundred yards or so without looking round. Then, turning on his back, and seeing the Italian pulling like a demon towards the island, he guessed his purpose, and laughed at his simplicity. Half a mile or more was no very wonderful distance to swim, in such lovely water too; and, so long as the fellow did not steal his money, the joke was enjoyable enough. But even in the lovely water of Lago Maggiore a swimmer may be seized with cramp; and the mad Englishman, trying in vain to rub down into their places the knotted muscles of his calf, spun round and round in his agony, and finally sank, if not to the bottom, yet quite deep enough to insure his coming up again most effectually drowned.

"I have seen that face before," said Tom Pippin, when the body was brought up to the door of his hotel. "That's Cuffs, the policeman. I'll swear to him. Does any one know where he lived?"

A small pension some little distance down the road was pointed out as the place from whence the mad Englishman had last been seen to issue; and Tom immediately set out thither, with the good-natured intention of breaking the sad news to Mrs. Cuffs more tenderly than it would probably be communicated by the Italian boatman or the landlord, and with a very decided curiosity to discover for himself how far his uncle's recently-formed suspicions were just, and whether or not Mr. Cuffs had been a good man and true.

Mrs. Cuffs was nursing a baby. Of course Tom did not know one baby from another, and was wholly unprepared to swear that the child which lay croaking in the sickly-looking woman's arms was his own cousin. Mrs. Cuffs might have half a dozen babies of her own, for all Tom could tell; but it could do no harm, and might do a world of good, to make believe for once that he was very wise.

"Aw—Mrs. Cuffs, I presume," said Tom.

"Some mistake, sir," replied the sickly woman.

"By Jove, then it's aw your mistake, not mine," said Tom. "I'll trouble you aw to hand over that baby. His mother, Lady Appletree, aw, wants him back again."

Down went the sickly woman like a shot, the baby falling with her on the floor. Tom took the child, and held it, to the best of his belief, the right way upwards. But, when the sickly woman came to herself, the child proved to be upside down; though Tom afterwards declared that, when the poor little thing had been righted, he couldn't for the life of him see any difference.

Mrs. Cuffs found it hard to keep up appearances, after having fainted straight away at the first breath of an accusation laid against her. Nevertheless, she began some plausible tale, which she and the detective had rehearsed together, and which her visitor took for what it was worth.

Then Tom had *his* tale to tell ; and, before the telling of it was fairly over, the woman was at his feet, confessing the whole plot from the very first, weeping for her own and her husband's guilt, weeping for the mother whom she had robbed, and praying earnestly that Tom would deal gently with her, remembering that her own breasts had fed the child.

Tom sent her to Milan, where she declared that she could earn for herself a living in some honest trade ; and, having engaged an Italian maiden to look after the baby, he set off at once for England, traveling with the utmost speed that he thought an infant of nine months might safely bear. On the road he examined a pocket-book which he had found in the policeman's room, and which he rightly judged to contain important papers. Among them was the document drawn up in the cottage at Withycombe, the signature attached to which set Tom shuddering as he read it. "The villain !" muttered Tom ; "the unmitigated villain ! He shall break stones at Portland for the rest of his life, by George he shall ! No, he sha'n't—for the sake of that poor boy ! Well—I'll keep it to myself, and think it over."

Tom called at the house in Bolton Street, May-Fair, in case his uncle should happen to be in town ; and there he found the earl, thoroughly enjoying his own society, and solacing his loneliness with salmon and champagne.

"Aw," said Tom, announcing himself, and leaving the Italian maiden with her infant in the cab, "aw—thought I should find you here."

"Can't say I thought I should find *you* here," returned the earl. "Where upon earth have you been, sir? and what have you got to say for yourself, after making fools of the whole lot of us down at Crookleigh?"

"Aw—it *was* rather rum, wasn't it? But look here—I'll aw make a bargain. I'm doosid hungry; and, if you'll give me some dinner, I'll give you your boy." Then Tom fetched in the Italian maiden, and the earl went mad with joy.

By the first train in the morning they ran down together to Withycombe, where Lady Appletree had been solacing *her* loneliness with draughts from the black bottle beneath her chair, to an extent which threatened to bring the days of her ladyship's pilgrimage on earth to a swift and sudden end. "She's a good woman," said the earl, "and I haven't a fault to find—except one. She does drink most confoundedly. She'll be as drunk as a fish when we get down there." Sure enough she was; but the baby brought her senses back again; and she put away the bottle for two whole days.

"Tom," said the earl, "you are the best fellow that ever breathed, and you deserve to be made free. I'll pay your debts, old boy, and give you an allowance, if you will promise to settle down quietly at Ribstone and live within your means. You know, of course, that poor young Crookleigh died last month, and the duke a fortnight afterwards?''

"No!" said Tom in astonishment; "I never heard a word about either of them."

"Ah, well—they are both dead; and Lady Maria is the richest woman in England. You could have her now, Tom, if you chose. But I say, Tom, next time you change your mind in the middle of the service, you must not tell the parson that you'll be 'blest.' It is not good manners, Tom, and it is highly improper, too. The bishop was very much hurt; he was, indeed." And the old man roared with laughter at his recollection of the scene.

"Sir John been here lately?" asked Tom, opening the way for intelligence about the one of whom he most wished to hear.

"Cut me dead," replied the earl; "but I expect he'll come round in time. Cut me dead, the proud old beggar! Just like a Scotchman! And what do you suppose he cut me for?"

"Haven't the most distant notion," said Tom.

"Because, when old Rampion died, a week or two ago, I gave that poor beggar Toyle the living; and now he is going to marry Edith Montgomery; and Sir John swears it is all my fault.—Why, what ever is the matter with you, old fellow?"

"Not much," said Tom, recovering himself. "You hit me rather hard, that is all." And then he told the earl his story.

The earl gave him such comfort as he could, and sent him into Dumplington to arrange financial matters with his lawyer. Mr. Teasel and Tom Pippin were

closeted yet once again for three whole hours; and
when the interview was over, Tom and his man of business did *not* shake hands.

The Dumplington gossips were in luck.   During the
space of less than two years an earl had married his
cook; a baby lord had been mysteriously stolen and
mysteriously brought home; a wedding in high life
had been interrupted at the altar itself; the very grammar-school had contributed its tragedy; and a marquis
and a duke had died.   Now there burst upon the ancient city yet another sensational report.   Mr. Peter
Teasel, of the Close, attorney-at-law, had sailed, as it
were in the middle of the night, for Melbourne, with
his wife and all his family, excepting only the eldest
boy, who was going to a private tutor to be crammed
for Woolwich, at the expense of an unknown friend.

CHAPTER XIII.

COALS OF FIRE.

WHEN Tom Pippin had concluded his financial arrangements with the lawyer, he did not visit, as usual, his friends at the schoolhouse—for in truth he had no friends there. The forty stripes inflicted upon one pupil, and the fatal accident which had befallen another, proved damaging to the prosperity of the farm. A terrible reaction set in against the excellent schoolmaster; boy after boy was, on one pretext or another, quietly withdrawn from Mrs. Goggs's motherly protection; and on the arrival of the second quarter-day after the receipt of his valentine the reverend gentleman's once flourishing household consisted of himself and his devoted wife; Goggs major, minor, and minimus, with their two small sisters; an invaluable cook; two willing domestics; a much-enduring shoeblack; and twelve founder's boys.

Mr. Goggs had come to poverty, and did not like it. It was a picturesque and useful theme for a discourse on Sunday; but on Monday and Tuesday he preferred contemplating its beneficial results in the case of other people. The profits of two years' farming, even on the most economical principles, could not be very enormous; the official salary of five hundred pounds

would scarcely suffice to keep the establishment going;
and Mr. Goggs was poor.

His straitened circumstances, however, might have
been more cheerfully borne, but for a new calamity of
which they were the cause. The invalid wife with
nerves unstrung was beginning to bully him. She
made him eat cold mutton for breakfast, and would
not allow him a study fire. She sold the produce of
his garden—pears, strawberries, grapes, and all. She
tied up his asparagus in bundles before his very eyes,
and sent it to the market, together with bushels of nice
green peas, and lettuces innumerable, and cucumbers
by the yard. She scolded him in the face of the very
founder's boys. and told him he ought to be ashamed
of himself for coming to dinner in a pair of rusty copper-colored trousers and an old green school-coat.
And Mr. Goggs did not like it. It weighed down his
spirits. It crippled his academic energies. It pros-
trated him utterly. He set impositions and forgot to
ask for them. He had not even the heart to reproduce
his mild and venerable jokes in school.

With the single exception of the Special Correspondent, who is certainly unapproachable in his own peculiar line, there is nobody who makes such abortive
attempts to be funny as the schoolmaster. Virgil,
Horace, Euclid, the Latin grammar—all contribute
their well-known series as regularly as the lesson comes
round. It is an excusable weakness. Hearing boys
construe is dull work; and the man who omits to let
off a joke, at a time when his listeners are bound to
laugh at it, misses a great opportunity. For the witticisms of the Special Correspondent it is perhaps some-

what more difficult to apologize. This gentleman does not merely improve the occasion, as the schoolmaster does, by fertilizing such facetious thoughts as the subject before him chances to supply. He rushes headlong into wit; determined to let you see, at the very outset, that you are going to be amused. He boldly prefaces a sermon of six columns and a half with a text from Thackeray or Dickens, expanding the idea thus happily borrowed with a colloquial sprightliness, which shows you at once what a jovial larky sort of fellow he must be. "It is one of the Wellers, I forget which, who says, Nobody ever seed a dead donkey." You are, of course, much interested in being informed that, though the Special Correspondent cannot just now remember which of the Wellers it was, yet upon the whole he knows his Pickwick tolerably well. What perhaps you fail immediately to apprehend is the connection between the text and the discourse which follows. Another gentleman draws upon his recollections of *Punch*, illustrating his graphic account of a *sortie*, or a charge of cavalry, with one of John Leech's drawings. "Like the urchin who threw a stone at a window, and then said, Please, sir, it wasn't me; so the French troops, etc. etc." Here again, though to some extent you miss the point of the reminiscence, you are, nevertheless, gratified by the discovery that your entertainer is of a youthful turn of mind; and you admit, as a matter of bare justice, that a writer who cannot raise a smile by any pleasantries of his own does wisely when he calls to his aid the historical pleasantries of other people. In recounting, however, his personal adventures, the Special Correspondent has his subject more completely in hand. There is nothing forced about his witticisms then. He has no need to consult his Pickwick, or recall a sketch from the inexhaustible *Punch*. He has plenty to tell, and he is thoroughly at home in the telling of it. "I had just shaken hands with the crown prince, when I heard my name called out in a cheery voice; and, looking round, I recognized the Duke of Lancashire." In such a case as this we perceive at once the full significance of the fact recorded; we shrink back into our easy-chairs, abashed at our own utter unworthiness; and we peruse with more than wonted reverence the journal wherein we put our trust, whose Special Correspondent shakes hands with crown princes and is hailed by the Duke of Lancashire in cheery tone.

Mr. Goggs, however, was funny no longer. He drooped and languished, and pined away. He so palpably neglected his work that the trustees of Woodruff's Charity carried a vote of confidence against him; accepted his resignation of the farm; bestowed upon his three sons, in consideration of their father's services, appointments as founder's boys; and obtained for the schoolmaster himself the office of chaplain, and instructor of half-witted youth, at the Dumplingshire County Asylum.

Here Mr. Goggs did his best to go mad himself. He would neither eat nor drink; and his wife, with her bitter reproaches, would not let him sleep. All night long she taunted him with his self-inflicted ruin; and he, poor wretch, had not life enough left in him for a retort or a counter reproach, even in its most imbecile form. The story of his desolation was told, in

thrilling words, wherever Dumplington matron en-
countered Dumplington maid ; and Harry Northcote,
hearing of it in the Christmas holidays when he came
home from his new school, formed half a dozen im-
practicable schoolboy plots for his unfortunate cousin's
relief.

"I was sure that you would want to do something
for him," said the captain, laughing at the wildness of
Harry's schemes, "and so I put off doing anything
myself until the holidays. But you know, my dear
boy, you can't upset a man's will, and take half of
what he leaves you and pour the other half bodily into
another man's lap."

"But that's just what I want to do, all the same,"
said Harry. "I have quite made up my mind that he
shall have the twenty thousand pounds; and surely,
papa, it might be managed somehow."

"He is welcome to it, as far as I am concerned,"
said the captain, "but I am not at all sure that he will
take it from either you or me ; and, what is more, I
don't see how we are to offer it, without getting into
some frightful mess with the lawyers."

The lawyers, however, proved reasonable, and were
graciously pleased to permit that Harry should spend
his own money as he pleased. It appeared that the
legacy had been paid by old Mr. Barroll's executors to
Captain Northcote, as guardian of the legatee ; and
that if the captain chose to present his young ward
with twenty thousand pounds during his minority, nobody could prevent him. Of course he had no legal
right to do so, and Harry, on coming of age, might
make him pay it all over again ; but the father would

take his chance of this, without any very serious mis-
givings as to the claims which might be made upon
him hereafter by the young heir. So Harry, accompanied by his darling Grab, who was spending his
Christmas at Aleworth, rode off to the asylum and inquired for the Rev. Mr. Goggs.

The Rev. Mr. Goggs was in a bad way. His garments were scarcely decent, and his person was osten-
tatiously unclean. The copper-colored trousers and
green school-coat had been pitiable enough ; but Harry
could not remember when he had ever seen his relative
in such a plight as he presented now. His room was a
den of discomforts, and his young visitor could hardly
breathe for the foulness of the air.

"Please, sir," began Harry, feeling his way to
business, and recollecting something of the schoolmaster's intense vanity, "please, sir, I have come to
beg your pardon for giving you so much trouble at
school. I am awfully sorry, really I am. I should not
play such a lot of tricks if I could have my time over
again."

"Have you supplicated pardon from on high?"
asked Mr. Goggs, turning his eyes toward heaven with
a gesture so devout, that Harry thought he must surely
be going up on high to receive the supplication.

"Well, no, sir—upon my word I haven't," replied
the boy, who was not quite prepared to let his penitence
go the length of a religious exercise.

"Then — let us pray !" said Mr. Goggs; "let
us——"

"Really, I am afraid I sha'n't have time to-day,"
interrupted Harry. "My father wants me to get back

to luncheon, and I have something particular to say. You won't be offended, sir, will you?"

"Well, what is it?" inquired Mr. Goggs, who looked as offended as a man need look already.

"I want you to do me a favor, sir," said Harry, blushing, and wondering how ever he should get over the ground with a man who came such a very little way to meet him.

"Well, Northcote, I am sure I don't know. I can make no promises. You must be aware that your behavior at school was not such as to give you any claim upon my regard. Your idleness, *and* stubbornness, *and* ingratitude to Mrs. Goggs and myself were altogether reprehensible; and I can only express my surprise that you should have had the hardihood to intrude yourself upon me."

"Intrude, indeed!" said Mrs. Goggs, sneaking into the room. "I'll intrude him! What do you mean, Northcote, by your impudence in coming here? If Mr. Goggs had an atom of spirit in him, he would kick you out at the door. Now, sir, just you march, and your precious dog after you."

"Grab won't hurt anybody, ma'am," said Harry, apologetically. "I told him to stop outside with the pony."

"And *I* told somebody to bring him *inside*, and give the poor thing a plate of bones," returned Mrs. Goggs; "and all I can say is, that I hope he'll like them."

"Why, you don't mean to say——" began Harry.

"I mean to say, young man, that we don't want your company, nor your dog's either. You have

brought me and Mr. Goggs to ruin, by your disgrace-
ful conduct at school.   You are strutting about with a
fine fortune, which belongs by rights to us, and not to
you; and the sooner you make yourself scarce, the
better."

But Harry had made himself scarce, long before the
matron's rebuke came to an end.   There was something in the woman's manner when she spoke of the
plate of bones, which set the boy suspecting, incredi-
ble as the notion was, that she had done a mischief to
his dear dog.   He rushed down-stairs, therefore, and
into the yard where he had tied up his pony, but Grab
was certainly not there.   He opened every door which
seemed to lean into the building, but his favorite was
nowhere to be seen.   At last, attracted by strange,
unearthly cries, he ran down a passage, and into a
dreary-looking hall, where a score of half-witted lads
were grinning and croaking over a sight which a score
of devils, if they had been but sane, could hardly have
stood still to see.   The dog, swollen and shrunk by
turns, as he writhed in his agony, with the yellow foam
gushing out of his mouth, and his great, red tongue wagging itself from side to side; the dog—his dog—his dear,
dear Grab—lay dying on the floor, lashing the boards
with his feathery tail, and swinging himself round from
posture to posture with cries of torment that could not be
endured.   Harry flung himself on the ground, and threw
his arms around the creature's neck, as if he would
share his torment with him; but the torment was over
now.   Grab tried to lick his master, but the tongue
would not move; tried to give a paw, but the paw hung
stiffly down; looked all his undying love into the boy's

face, as he wished him, after his doggish fashion, a last good-by; and went to that happy place in the world unseen where the spirits of good dogs dwell.

The workhouse-master lent a horse and cart, and a workhouse-man to drive it as far as Aleworth; and Harry, wild with grief, rode his pony alongside. Before he started, however, he went again into Mr. Goggs's room, and made him understand, through his convulsive sobbings, what the real intention of his visit had been. "It is all yours," said the boy. "I sha'n't ever touch it. It's invested somewhere or other, my father says; but they will tell you all about it at the bank, and you can have it whenever you like."

"Very right and proper feeling," said the schoolmaster, patronizingly. "It is a satisfaction to me, my dear Northcote, to see that your heart is changed, and that you have profited by the lessons in godliness which you learned from me at Dumplington. I am sorry that your dog was poisoned by mistake; but I have no doubt that Mrs. Goggs will get you another."

Much comforted by this assurance, and by the gracious mode in which the schoolmaster had received his gift, Harry rode home, scarcely ever taking his eyes off the body of his murdered friend. At the lodge-gates he met Tom Pippin, who fairly tumbled off his saddle at the sight of Grab lying dead in a cart.

"I have seen your father," said Tom; "and he has told me all about this legacy business; and I won't say to you, Harry, what I told him in return. They have been very kind to you, Harry, both of them. They were very kind to your dearest schoolboy friend, and now they have been very particularly kind to your dog.

You are quite right to let them see that you are not ungrateful. Well, my boy, Tom Pippin doesn't brag much about his feelings, and it isn't very often that Tom Pippin has been seen to blub; but if Tom Pippin stands here much longer, with Harry Northcote on one side of him, and Grab, murdered in cold blood, on the other, why, somebody will have to——"

What somebody would have to do did not, however, immediately appear; for Tom, after shaking hands warmly with his friend, and patting yet once again the dog's shaggy coat, scrambled up into his saddle and rode hastily away, the tears streaming down his cheeks as they had not done since he was a little child.

But Tom had some more crying to do before he went to bed that night. When he reached home, he found a messenger from Crookleigh Castle, waiting to drive him over to see Lady Maria Bent before she died. The poor idiot had never quite recovered from the shock of Tom's eccentric behavior on her bridal morning. She felt it from the very first more deeply than she permitted any one to know; and a serious illness which seized her in the autumn had produced a succession of fits, so violent and so exhausting that recovery of strength was utterly impossible. The fits had left her now; but when Tom reached her bedside, and gazed with horror and self-reproach at a ruin which his own thoughtlessness had made, she was so intensely weak that she could scarcely summon breath enough to whisper to him her last few words.

"Don't cry, Tom," she said, as Tom flung himself on his knees and burst into tears. "Mine has not been such a happy life as to make my friends wish it might be spun out any longer. I've been a mistake down here, Tom. I shall do better where I am going. Oh, Tom! you shouldn't have done it before such a lot of people. But, bless you, Tom! I didn't care. Well, it is all over now. And I have left you all the money, Tom, every scrap of it. And you must keep it in remembrance of my great, great love—for no one ever loved as I have loved you. Don't go horse-racing with it, Tom. I want you to be kind to the people here, and look after them yourself, and not pay some fellow two thousand pounds a year to rob you and humbug you. And I should like to have my schools kept up, Tom, and some churches built where they are wanted. Ah, Tom, there's a deal to be done, if you will only stop at home and do it. Good-by, Tom. I think I may ask you to kiss me now, Tom. Good-by. I sha'n't forget you where I am going. Give me one kiss, and then I'll go."

So he kissed her; and, as he kissed her, angels came down and carried the poor, misshapen dwarf away to a land where the crooked shall be made straight again, and ugliness in man or woman shall be no more counted as a crime.

THE END.